IGINIO UGO TARCHETTI

Fantastic Tales

EDITED AND TRANSLATED BY

Lawrence Venuti

archipelago books

Racconti fantastici first published by Treves in 1869
This translation first published by Mercury House in 1992

Archipelago Books
232 3rd Street #A111
Brooklyn, NY 11215
www.archipelagobooks.org

Distributed by Penguin Random House
www.penguinrandomhouse.com

Cover art: *Becoming* by Mary Frank, courtesy of DC Moore Gallery.
Text design by Gopa & Ted2, Inc.

Library of Congress Cataloging-in-Publication Data
is available upon request

This book was made possible by the New York State Council on the Arts
with the support of Governor Andrew M. Cuomo and the New York
State Legislature. Funding for this book was provided by a grant from
the Carl Lesnor Family Foundation. Archipelago Books also gratefully
acknowledges the generous support of Lannan Foundation and the
New York City Department of Cultural Affairs.

PRINTED IN THE UNITED STATES

Contents

The Legends of the Black Castle   3

Captain Gubart's Fortune   25

A Spirit in a Raspberry   31

Bouvard   49

A Dead Man's Bone   89

The Lake of the Three Lampreys
(A Popular Tradition)   101

The Elixir of Immortality
(In Imitation of the English)   109

The Letter U
(A Madman's Manuscript)   135

The Fated   147

Fantastic Tales

The Legends of the Black Castle

I DO NOT KNOW whether the memoirs I am about to write can hold the interest of anyone but me—I write, at any rate, for myself. Nearly all of them refer to an event pervaded with mystery and terror, in which very often it will be impossible to trace the thread of a narrative, or infer a conclusion, or find any reason whatsoever. I alone will be able to do these things, I who am actor and victim at once. Begun at that age when the mind is susceptible to the strangest and most frightening hallucinations; continued, interrupted, and resumed after an interval of almost twenty years; encompassed by all the apparitions of dreams; completed—if such can be said of something that had no obvious beginning—in a land that was not mine and to which I had been drawn by traditions filled with superstition and gloom, I can only consider this the most inscrutable event in my life, an insoluble enigma, the shadow of a fact, a revelation that remains incomplete yet eloquently expressive of a past existence. Were they facts, or visions? Both—or perhaps neither. In the abyss that swallows up the past, no facts or ideas endure; there is merely the past. The

mighty characters of things are destroyed, like the things themselves, and with them ideas suffer transmutations—truth lies only
in the instant—past and future are deep shadows enveloping us
on all sides, amidst which, leaning on our escort, the present, as if
detached from time, we make the painful journey of life.

Yet did we have a previous life? Have we already lived out our
current existence in another epoch, with a different heart and a
different destiny? Was there a moment in time when we resided
in places we now avoid, loved creatures whom death snatched
away years ago, lived among people whose works we see today,
or whose memory we pursue in chronicles or obscure traditions?
I have no definitive answers to these questions. And yet for all
that . . . yes, I have often heard something speak to me of a
past life, something murky and confused, I admit, but distant,
infinitely distant. I possess certain memories that cannot be contained within the narrow bounds of my life; to reach their origin,
I must retrace the curve of years, journey back very far . . . two or
three centuries . . . Before today, too, I frequently had occasion
to linger in some countryside on my travels and exclaim, "I must
have already seen this place. I was here, several times . . . These
fields, this valley, this horizon—I recognize them!" And who
has not declared now and then, thinking that he has recognized
a familiar countenance in some person, "That man, I have seen
him before. Where? When? Who is he? I cannot be definite, but

surely we have seen one another before, we know one another!"
In my childhood, I often saw an old man I certainly knew when
he was a boy, and who certainly knew me when I was quite old;
we did not converse but rather looked at one another like people
who sense that they have met. Along a road to Poole, near the
beach at Manica, I found a stone where I vividly recall sitting,
about seventy years ago, and I remember that it was a dreary, rainy
day and I was waiting for someone whose name and face I have
forgotten, but who was dear to me. In an art gallery at Graz, I saw
a portrait of a woman I loved, and I recognized her immediately,
even though she was younger then, and the portrait was painted
perhaps twenty years after our separation. The canvas bore the
date 1647. Most of these memoirs go back roughly to that period.

There was a time in my boyhood when I could not listen to
the cadence of certain songs the country women sang to us on
the farms without feeling suddenly transported to an epoch so
remote from my life that I could not reach it if I multiplied my
present age many, many times. I had only to hear that melody to
lapse instantly into a condition like paralysis, a spiritual lethargy
that made everything around me seem strange, whatever my state
of mind when it overtook me. After twenty years, I have never
again experienced that phenomenon. Did I never hear the melody
again? Or has my spirit, already quite inseparable from my current
existence, become deaf to the call?

Either my nature is infirm, or my thinking differs from other men's, or they undergo the same sensations, but without realizing it. I feel, yet am unable to express how, that my life—or what we properly use this term to designate—did not begin with the day of my birth and will not end at my death; I feel this with the same force, with the same fullness of sensation that I feel life at this instant, although in a way that is more obscure, stranger, more inexplicable. On the other hand, how do we feel that we are *living* at this instant? One says, *I am alive*. But this is not sufficient: when we sleep, we have no awareness of existing—and nonetheless we live. This awareness of existing cannot be fully circumscribed by the narrow boundaries of what we call life. We can contain two lives: this belief, in various forms, has been accepted by every people in every period. One life is essential, continuous, perhaps imperishable, whereas the other is changeable, progressing by fits and starts, more or less brief, more or less recurrent. One is essence; the other relevation, form. What dies in the world? Life dies, but the spirit, the secret, the force of life does not die: it lives forever in the world.

I mentioned sleep. And what is sleep? Can we be so certain that sleep is not a separate life, an existence detached from waking? What happens to us in that state? Who can say? The events in dreams where we are witnesses or participants—could they be real? Could what we call by this term be no more than a confused memory of those events? . . . A frightening and terrible thought! Perhaps we, in a different order of things, participate in actions, feelings, ideas of which we cannot retain any awareness in our waking lives; we live in another world and among other beings whom we daily leave and meet again. Every evening one life dies; every night another is born. But what happens to these partial existences may also happen to that inner, more precisely defined existence that comprehends them. Men always turn their gaze to the future, never the past; the end, never the beginning; the effect, never the cause. All the same, the portion of life to which time can neither remove nor add anything, where our mind has a great right to settle, and from whose investigation it could derive the highest satisfactions and the most useful teachings the life spent in a more or less remote past. We have lived, we live, we shall live. There are some lacunae among these existences, but they will be filled. An epoch will arrive when the entire mystery will be revealed to us; when the spectacle of life, whose threads originate and vanish in eternity, will unfold completely before our eyes; when we shall read, as in a divine book, the works, thoughts, ideas conceived or executed in a past existence or in a series of partial existences that we have forgotten. I do not know whether other men will keep this faith; that, in any case, can neither strengthen nor undermine my conviction.

But here is my story.

In 1830, I was fifteen years old and was living with my family in a large village in the Tyrol, whose name I am forced to withhold for several personal reasons. Not more than three generations had passed since my ancestors came to find work in that village. Although they certainly arrived from Switzerland, the direct line of the family was of German descent. The memories that remained of its beginnings were so inexact and obscure that I was never afforded the opportunity to draw very precise deductions. I am, in any case, concerned only to ascertain this fact, that my family was of German stock.

There were five of us. My father and mother were born in that village and received there the limited, modest education appropriate to the petty bourgeoisie. My family possessed some aristocratic traditions, however, traditions whose origins go back to Old Saxon feudalism. Yet the fortune of our house was so paltry that it repressed all our impulses of ambition and pride. My family's customs did not differ in any way from those of the humblest families among the common people: my parents had been born and raised among them; their life was a completely blank page. Neither from their society nor from their manner of education could I derive any of those ideas or childhood memories that predispose one to superstition and terror.

The only personage whose life contained something mysterious and inscrutable and who came to join my family, in a sense, was an old uncle said to be bound to us by common interests. I have, however, been entirely unable to decipher the rational grounds of these interests since I came into possession of my family's fortune at his and my father's deaths.

My uncle had reached ninety years of age then—I am speaking of that period from which these memoirs of mine date. He was a tall, imposing figure, although slightly stooped; his facial features were majestic, prominent, I would say almost chiseled; his gait was proud although unsteady from age, his eyes restless and searching, doubly alive in that face whose mobility and expression the years had paralyzed. When he was still young, he had embraced a career in the priesthood, driven by the insistent pressures of his family. Later, he laid aside the cassock and devoted himself to the military; the French Revolution found him in its regiments. He spent forty-two years away from his country, and when he returned—since he had not broken his vows in the Church—he again took up the cassock, which he wore without blemish or pious affectation until his death. He was known to be endowed with a quick yet habitually calm temperament, an indomitable will, and a vast, erudite mind, although he may have done his utmost not to show it. Capable of lofty passions and exceptional courage, he was esteemed as an extraordinary man, a noble, outstanding figure. What helped to invest him with this prestige, moreover, was the mystery that concealed his past: a few rumors referred to numerous strange events wherein he was said to have participated. He had certainly performed important services for the Revolution; what services and with what influence he performed them will never be known: he died when he was ninety-six, carrying the secret of his life to the grave.

Everyone knows the customs of village life; I shall not restrain myself from discoursing upon those that were specific to my family. Every winter evening we used to gather in a vast room on the ground floor and sit in a circle around one of those large fireplaces, so ancient and so comfortable but now abolished by modern taste, which has substituted small coal stoves for them. My uncle, who lived in a separate apartment in the same house, sometimes came to join our gatherings, when he would recount adventures from his travels or scenes from the Revolution that filled us with terror and amazement. He was always silent about himself, however, and when asked of the role he played, he diverted the narrative from the subject.

One evening—I remember it as if it were yesterday—we assembled in that room as usual. It was winter, but there was no snow; the frozen, frost-whitened ground reflected the rays of the moon, producing a vibrant white light like an aurora. Everything was silent, and you could hear only the irregular hammering of some drops that trickled down from the icicles on the drainpipes. All of a sudden, our conversation was interrupted by the unexpected dull thud of an object thrown into the courtyard from the low perimeter wall. My father rose, went out, and hastened to the gate, which opens onto the street. But he heard nothing more than the noise of some footsteps and saw, down the broad expanse of street stretching before him, only a few people walking away. Then he picked up a small box that had been thrown on the ground and returned to the room with it. We all gathered around him to examine it. Instead of a box, it turned out to be a huge square bundle, wrapped in old, grayish, rust-stained paper and stitched along the sides with white thread at exact and regular intervals—a feature that declared the office of a woman's hand. The paper, cut here and there by the thread, reddened and worn at the edges, indicated that the bundle had been made some time ago.

My uncle received it from my father's hands, and I saw him tremble and blanch as he examined it. The paper was cut, and he drew out two dusty old volumes. No sooner had he glanced over them than a cadaverous pallor came over his face, and concealing a more profound feeling of grief and amazement, he said, "How strange!" After a brief moment during which none of us dared speak, he resumed, "It is a manuscript, two volumes of memoirs dating back to the very beginnings of our family. They contain several of our most glorious traditions. I gave these two volumes to a young man who, although he was not a member of our immediate family, was related to us by certain ties which I cannot now reveal. They were the pledge for a promise that time, not I, has prevented me from keeping: yes, time . . . ," he added to himself in a low voice. "I knew him at the University of _____, when he was studying theology there; he was guillotined on the Place de la Grève, and his family was destroyed by the Revolution, it must be forty years ago now . . . not one of them survived . . . How strange!"

After a short interval, he noticed that a very fine reddish dust had accumulated in the pages, and as if recalling some danger, he told us, "Wash your hands."

"Why?"

"Nothing . . . "

We obeyed. The rest of the evening was spent in silence. My uncle was given to sad thoughts, and one could see that he was trying hard to evoke or drive away some very painful memories. He retired quite early, shut himself in his apartment, and remained there for two days before he appeared again.

That night I went to bed prey to strange, frightening thoughts without knowing quite why. I was more troubled by the idea of that incident than a boy of my age should have been. It would be pointless for me now to attempt to render in words the inexplicable, singular sentiments that stirred within me at that moment. I felt that those two volumes, my uncle, and myself were caught in a web of mysterious, distant relations I had never noticed till then, relations whose nature I could not decipher by any means, and whose end I could not understand. They were, or they seemed to me, memories. But whose? I did not know. From what period? They were remote. In my youthful intelligence everything was altered and confused.

I slept under the impression of those ideas and had this dream.

I was twenty-five. It was as if my mind were crowded with all the ideas, experiences, lessons that time would have made me endure over the years to mark the difference between the fantasy of adolescence and the waking reality of adulthood. Nonetheless, I remained alien to this process of maturation, even though I comprehended it. I felt in myself all the intellectual growth of that age, but I judged it with the discrimination and opinions proper to my fifteen years. There were two individuals within me, one belonging to action, the other to the consciousness and evaluation of action. It was a simultaneity of effect, one of those contradictions or oddities peculiar only to dreams.

I found myself in a broad valley flanked by two tall mountains. The vegetation, the farming, the shape and arrangement of the cabins, and something inexplicably different, something ancient in the light, in the atmosphere, in everything that surrounded me said that I was in an epoch very remote from my actual existence—two or three centuries away, at least. But how did that happen? How did I come to be in these fields? I did not know. Yet it was natural in the dream: I knew that certain events had justified my stopping in that place, but I did not know what they were; I was not conscious of their value, their importance, only of their existence. I was alone and sad. I was walking for a definite reason, fixed beforehand, some purpose that drew me to that place, but of which I was ignorant. High over the far end of the valley rose a sheer cliff, perpendicular, massive, grooved with cracks from which not one liana sprouted. At its summit stood a castle that commanded the entire valley, and that castle was black. Its towers were protected by crossbows and filled with soldiers, the gates of its bridges were lowered, its turrets were packed with men and weapons of defense. Locked inside its inner rooms was a woman of prodigious beauty whom, in the consciousness of the dream, I knew as "the lady of the black castle." That woman was bound to me by a long-standing affection, and I had to defend her, had to deliver her from the castle. But down in the valley, at the base of the rock where I had stopped, an object painfully caught my attention: on the steps of a tomb sat a man who had just then left the castle. He was dead but still living; he presented a totality of things impossible to describe, the coupling of death and life, the rigidity, the nothingness of the one tempered by the sensitivity, the essence of the other. His eyes, which I knew had been blinded by a red-hot nail, were pierced by two small square holes that made him appear simultaneously terrible and pitiful. Bloody memories were linked to that deed, memories of a crime in which I had taken part. Inexplicable relationships joined me, him, and the lady of the castle. He looked at me with his pierced eyes, and by means of a gesture and a kind of will that he did not manifest, but that I somehow read in him, he incited me to free the lady.

A path carved into the side of the cliff led to the castle. An immense quantity of projectiles hurled from the mangonels on the towers hindered me from reaching it. Yet how strange! All of those enormous projectiles struck me without killing me—nonetheless, they stopped me. I saw the lady through the walls of the castle: she was alone, rushing through her rooms, her black hair unbound, her face and dress white as snow, stretching out her arms to me with an expression of desire and infinite pity. And I followed her with my eyes through all those rooms, which I recognized: I had once lived there with her. That sight encouraged me to run to her aid, but I could not; the projectiles hurled from the towers hindered me. At every turn in the path, the shower grew denser and more ferocious, and there were many turns— after this one, another, after that one, still another . . . I rose and rose . . . The lady called me from the castle, looked out of the broad windows, her hair raining down on her breast, beckoned me with her hand to hurry, spoke words full of sweetness and love, but I could not reach her—my impotence was agonizing. How long that terrible struggle lasted I cannot say—for the entire duration of the dream, all through the night . . .

Finally, I arrived at the doors of the castle, although I did not know by what means. They stood undefended; the soldiers had vanished. The closed doors swung open wide by themselves, creaking on their rusty hinges, and in the black recesses of the entry hall I saw the lady with her long white train, running toward me with open arms, traveling the distance that separated us with astonishing rapidity, scarcely grazing the floor. She hurled herself into my arms with the abandon of a corpse, with the lightness, the assent of an object that was hollow, flexible, supernatural. Her beauty was unearthly; her voice was pleasant, but faint as the echo of a note; her eyes, dark and veiled as if she had just been weeping, pierced the most hidden depths of my soul, although without wounding it, in fact investing it with her light as by the effect of some radiance. We spent several minutes locked in this embrace; a delight I have never felt before or after that moment coursed through all my nerves. For an instant I experienced the full intoxication of the embrace without realizing it. Yet no sooner did I pause over this thought, no sooner did the consciousness of the delight descend upon me than I witnessed a terrible transformation in her. The delicately rounded figure I felt trembling in my hands flattened out, contracted, disappeared, and in my fingers, caught in the folds that suddenly formed in her dress, grasped the bones of a skeleton protruding here and there . . . Quaking I lifted my eyes and saw her face turn pale, thin, lose its flesh, bend beneath my mouth, and a lipless grin gave me a desperate kiss, long, parched, terrible . . . Then a quiver, a deathly shudder ran down my spine. I attempted to disengage myself from her arms, to push her away . . . and in the violence of the act my sleep was broken—I woke in tears, screaming.

I returned to my fifteen years, to my adolescent ideas and opinions, my puerilities. The entire dream seemed to me much more strange, much more incomprehensible, than frightening. What were the sentiments that seized me in that state? I had yet to experience the pleasure of a kiss, had not even thought about love, and could not account for the sensations I felt that night. Nevertheless, I was sad, possessed by an unyielding thought; it seemed to me that the dream was not in fact a dream, but a memory, a confused idea about things, the recollection of an incident very remote from my present life.

On the following night I had another dream.

Once again I found myself in that place, but everything was changed. The sky, trees, roads were no longer the same; the flanks of the cliffs were crossed by paths covered with honeysuckle; of the castle there remained only some ruins, and hemlock and nettles grew in the deserted courtyards and the crevices of the ground-floor rooms. When I passed near the tomb that had previously stood in the valley and was now no more than a few stones, the blind man was again sitting there, on a step that was still intact. He offered me a bloodstained handkerchief and said, "Bring it to the lady of the castle." I found myself seated in the ruins; the lady of the castle was at my side. We were alone. There was no sound of a voice, an echo, a rustle of branches in the field. Grasping my hands, she told me, "I have come from so far away to see you again. Listen to how my heart is beating . . . Listen to how loudly my heart is beating! . . . Feel my forehead and my breast. Oh, I am so weary, I ran so fast! I am exhausted from the long wait . . . It has been almost three hundred years since I last saw you."

"Three hundred years!"

"Do you not remember? We were together in this castle. But they are terrible memories! Let us not recall them."

"That would be impossible; I have forgotten them."

"You shall remember them after your death."

"When?"

"Very soon."

"When?"

"In twenty years, on the twentieth of January: our destinies, like our lives, cannot be reunited before that day."

"And what then?"

"Then we shall be happy; we shall realize our vows."

"Which?"

"You shall remember them in due course . . . you shall remember everything. Your expiation is about to end: you have passed through eleven lives before arriving at this one, which is your last. I passed through only seven; forty years have already elapsed since I completed my pilgrimage in the world. You shall complete yours after the twenty years remaining in this last life. But I cannot linger with you any longer; it is necessary for us to separate."

"First explain this enigma to me."

"That is impossible . . . Yet perhaps you need to understand it. Yesterday I threw his promise in his face; I restored half of it to you, those two volumes, those memoirs you wrote, those pages so full of affection . . . you shall have them, if that man who was then so fatal to us does not stop you from having them.

"Who?"

"Your uncle . . . he . . . the man of the valley."

"He? My uncle!"

"Yes, did you see him?"

"I saw him, and he sends you this bloodied handkerchief by me."

"It is your blood, Arturo," she said, transported. "Heaven be praised! He has kept his promise."

As the lady of the castle said these words, she disappeared, and I awoke terrified.

My uncle was still shut up in his apartment. As soon as he reappeared, I rushed into his rooms to get hold of those volumes, but I found only a heap of ashes: he had fed them to the flames. Yet my terror rose when I stirred the ashes and discovered several fragments that seemed written in my own hand! From the few disconnected words that remained intelligible and with a powerful exertion of my memory, I could reconstruct entire sentences that referred to the events obscurely hinted in my dreams. I could no longer doubt the truth of the revelations; and although I never succeeded in recalling all my memories to disperse the shadows that spread over those facts, it was no longer possible for me to gainsay their existence. The black castle was often mentioned in the fragments, which also touched briefly on the passionate love that seemed to bind me to the lady and the criminal suspicion that hung over the man of the valley. Furthermore, by a coincidence that was as singular as it was frightening, the night on which I had the dream was precisely the night of the twentieth of January: exactly twenty years, then, remained until my death.

Since that day I have never forgotten the prediction; yet although I did not doubt that there was a foundation of truth in the entire collection of facts, I succeeded in persuading myself that my youth, my sensitivity, my imagination had done a great deal to cloak them with authority. My uncle, who died six years later while I was away from the family, never made the smallest revelation concerning those events. I did not have any more dreams that could be considered an explanation or continuation of them; and new feelings, new concerns, new passions came to distract me from that thought, establishing a new state of affairs and a new order of ideas to banish my sad, painful worry.

It was only nineteen years later that I persuaded myself, by incontrovertible evidence, that everything I had dreamt and witnessed was real, and that consequently the prediction of my death must come true.

In the year 1849, while traveling in the north of France, I made my way down the Rhine very close to its confluence with the little River Meuse and stopped to hunt in the countryside. Wandering alone one day along the lower slopes of a small chain of hills, I suddenly found myself in a valley where I seemed to have been on other occasions. No sooner did I have this thought than a terrible memory case a dull, frightening light in my mind, and I knew that this was the valley of the castle, the theater of my dreams and my past existence. Although everything had changed, although the fields, deserted before, were now golden with grain, and what remained of the castle were only some ruins half-buried in ivy, I immediately recognized the place, and thousands of memories, never before evoked, crowded into my troubled soul at that instant.

I asked a shepherd what the ruins might be, and he replied, "They are the ruins of the black castle. Are you familiar with the legend of the black castle? Truly, there are many legends about it, and they are not told by everyone in the same way; but if you wish to know the legend as I know it, if—"

"Tell it, tell it," I interrupted him, as I sat down on the grass at his side. And from him I learned a terrible story, a story that I shall never reveal (even though others may learn it in the same way) and on the basis of which I have reconstructed the entire edifice of my previous existence.

When he finished, I was barely able to drag myself to a small nearby village, whence I was conveyed, already ill, to Wiesbaden, and here I have been laid up in bed for three months.

Today, before departing, I induced myself to revisit the ruins of the castle. It is the first day of September; six months are left until the time of my death—six months, less ten days—since I do not doubt that I shall die on the appointed date. I have conceived the strange desire that some memory of me should remain. Seated on one of the castle stones, I endeavored to summon up all the distant circumstances of this event, and it was there that I wrote these pages in a fit of tremendous terror.

The author of these memoirs, who was my friend and a literary man of some note, continued on his journey to the interior of Germany and died on the twentieth of January in 1850, according to the prediction he received, murdered by a band of gypsies in the so-called gorges of Giessen near Freiburg.

I found these pages among his many manuscripts and published them.

[1867]

Captain Gubart's Fortune

NOTHING IN THIS world is more fickle, irrational, or singular than fortune. Every man has made it the subject of extravagant speculations and grand dreams, pursuing it indefatigably in casinos or in that noble institution known as the lottery. But fortune is generally found only where it is not sought. It loves unspirited lovers, the simpleminded, and the inconstant. The following incident is designed in part to demonstrate this truth.

In 1802, Gubart was a violinist, but a very bad one. Nature had not made him for the arts. Even though he was a fine young man and had learned to write and count, his suit of ticking, patched at the elbows and knees, betrayed his condition. Poor Gubart! He was born a lazy beggar, took a wife when he reached sixteen, and had three sons. One night, there was nothing for supper in Gubart's house, and these fasts were not growing any less frequent. His wife thrust his violin into his hands and said to him, "Gubart, go and play, please, try to scrape together some change for these children. And may God give you good fortune."

Gubart reluctantly took his violin and looked at it rudely. Between player and instrument there existed a kind of coldness, a long-standing grudge. Gubart considered the violin an enemy: no matter how many times he ventured out with it, everyone avoided him, and that never happened to him when he was alone. His resentment, therefore, was not entirely unfounded. His wife's usual remedy for beguiling the children's impatient hunger during his absence was to tell them some frightening tales about fairies, sorcerers, metamorphoses. In this way, spirit sometimes won a complete victory over matter, and since on that evening Gubart's three fortunate heirs were making rather nasty sneers and contortions, suggesting that they were not very far from the limit of their impatience, their good mother told them a most beautiful and curious little story, which, we regret to say, has not been faithfully preserved in the chronicle. At the most beautiful moment in the story, Gubart's wife was interrupted by two knocks on the door. "My God," she said, "this can't be my husband back already; he is so fast tonight," and she ran to open it, interpreting his speed in an extremely unfavorable way. But what a surprise! It was not Gubart at all, but an elegant usher from the palace wearing a uniform with gold-braided epaulettes and a hat with royal insignia. He was holding a large letter in both hands, and, what seemed even more strange, he looked drunk and was finding it difficult to maintain the customarily serious attitude of an usher.

"Does Gaetano Gubart live here?"

"He is my husband, but he is not at home."

"OK," continued the usher, "you will deliver this envelope to him as soon as he returns."

Gubart's wife took it with trembling hand; she usually worried about her husband. What could he have done this time? Who wrote this letter? What consequences would it bring? She asked herself these and other similar questions and joined them with the most bizarre conjectures. The little family's peace had been decidedly disturbed. The children, having broken off their neutrality, were energetically calling for their supper when another knock was heard at the door, and this time it was precisely Gubart returning. He was carrying two large loaves of bread. He had turned in a good performance and was somewhat reconciled with his violin. The screams and tears, the species of civil war in the family, were things that happened every evening, so he was not in the least surprised by them. Yet he was definitely amazed when his wife took him by the hand with an unusual air and asked him, almost tenderly, "Dear Gubart, my husband, what have you done? Confess everything, tell your wife at least. Here is a huge letter that was brought by an usher from the royal palace; read it at once, please."

This time Gubart was truly astonished. He broke the seal with veneration, removed from the envelope a sheet of paper folded four times, opened it, brought over a large candle, and read it aloud, although not without several interruptions.

"His Majesty Ferdinand IV, King of the Two Sicilies, etc., etc., having taken into consideration the important services rendered by Signor Gaetano Gubart during the recent disturbances in the kingdom, has seen fit to appoint him to the rank of captain in the infantry, assigning him at the same time to the 4th regiment of the army. Naples, 14 March 1802."

The wife and three sons were stupefied and remained speechless for some time.

Finally, the violinist, like the profound thinker he was, broke the silence and said, "It is obvious that the usher must have made a mistake. Another Gaetano Gubart must exist in this city; and this fact is so clear that it is pointless to abandon ourselves to vain hopes. Yet not for nothing did fortune bring about this error and this coincidence in names. I possess a very important letter, after all, and I can take advantage of it. My wife, take that old suit of clothes down from the cupboard, the one I bought around the time of our wedding: it must need some mending . . . Yes, of course, I myself will go see the king, and I hope my decision will not prove fruitless."

Gubart's house was humble; it consisted of one room, and on that evening a profound silence reigned there. His wife stayed awake deep into the night mending the wedding suit, and Gubart slept. Who can imagine what dreams were passing through his mind? . . .

The king had spent a miserable night, he was in his worst humor, and if a large hunting party had not been arranged for that day, it would have been impossible to see him.

But he was coming down the stairs when he heard the loud conversation Gubart was having with the palace guards. "By God," Gubart was saying, "let me pass, I want to talk with the king, he has appointed me captain." At that moment, the king reached the last step and, turning to the ushers, made a certain face that signified, Who is this person? What is the meaning of this uproar? "Your Majesty," said the head porter, "we are not to blame. This man was once a terrible violinist; now he has gone insane as well and says that he has been made a captain."

"Of course," interrupted Gubart, "but I suspect that the king has made an error. Here is the letter I received last night." King Ferdinand took the letter, read it, and understood everything. Yet since as a rule he wanted to maintain the belief that the supposed royal infallibility was intact, he mitigated the whiplash about to fall on poor Gubart's shoulders and, barely controlling his contempt, said, "Knave, who taught you to suspect that kings make mistakes? You have twelve hours left to reach your regiment."

This was Gubart's great fortune. But it is rare that a change in the status of one individual does not also produce a contrary change in another. The unfortunate usher who had carried the order that night—and who a few hours earlier had drunk several glasses of Salerno in the old Rosa wineshop—spent ten years in the dungeons of the Ovo prison: four for his conviction and six for attempted escape. He was released poor and sickly and died a beggar.

On the other hand, since ignorance of how to play the violin does not exclude presence of mind and an ordinary quantity of wit, and since Gubart was a very good boy and had much of both, he quickly passed through many ranks, had a huge family that enjoyed the king's favor, and lived happy and honored ever after.

This incident, despite its definite resemblance to those famous Arabian tales, is indisputably true and well known.

[1865]

A Spirit in a Raspberry

IN 1854, a prodigious event terrified and astonished the humble people who lived in a small village in Calabria.

I shall attempt to relate this amazing occurrence with the greatest possible exactness, although one must understand that exhibiting it in all its truth and with all its most interesting details is an extremely difficult task.

The young Baron B.—I regret that a solemn vow prohibits me from revealing his name—had recently inherited his paternal grandfather's rich and extensive barony, situated in one of the most enchanting areas of Calabria. The young heir had never been away from those mountains, with their abundance of orchards and game. In the old ancestral manor, which was once a fortified feudal castle, the family tutor taught him the rudiments of writing and the titles of three or four Latin classics from which he could cite, as the need arose, several well-known distiches. Like all southern Italians, he had a passion for hunting, horses, and love—three passions that often seem to walk in unison, like three good post-horses—and he could satisfy them when he pleased, without ever giving them a second thought; nor did he ever imagine that beyond the jagged peaks of the Apennines might lie other lands, with different men, and different passions.

However, since knowledge is not one of the essential requisites for happiness—and in fact seems opposed to it—the young Baron B. felt himself completely happy with the simple store of his verses; and no less happy with him were his domestic servants, his women, his bloodhounds, and his twelve green-liveried footmen, who were charged with running before and after his luxurious carriage on formal occasions.

A few months before the period in which our narrative is set, a single, doleful event brought grief to a family employed in domestic service and altered the peaceful usages of the castle. One of the baron's maids, a girl who was known to have had amorous intrigues with several servants, suddenly disappeared from the village; all the searches were in vain; and while not a few suspicions hung over one of the woodsmen—a young man with a violent temperament who had once taken a fancy to her, although without its being reciprocated—these suspicions were in reality so vague and unfounded that the young man's calm and confident demeanor was more than sufficient to dispel them.

This mysterious disappearance, which seemed to suggest the idea of a crime, had deeply saddened the honorable Baron B. But gradually he forgot about it, distracting himself with love and hunting. Joy and tranquility returned to the castle; the green-liveried footmen resumed their pranks in the anterooms; and two months had not yet passed before neither the baron nor any of his servants recalled the girl's disappearance.

It was now the month of November.

One morning, Baron B. awoke slightly troubled by a bad dream, jumped out of bed, threw open the window, and seeing that the sky was serene and his bloodhounds were sadly pacing the courtyard, pawing the door to go out, he said, "I want to go hunting, on my own. I notice several flocks of wild doves have gathered down there in the sown field; I shall see to it that they settle accounts with their wings." Having made this resolution, he finished getting dressed, slipped into his waterproof boots, slung his rifle diagonally across his shoulders, dismissed the two footmen who usually accompanied him, and went out surrounded by all his dogs, who, shaking their heads and flapping their broad ears, repeatedly thrust themselves between his legs, caressing his boots with their long tails.

Baron B. headed straight for the place where he had seen the wild doves alight. It was in the sowing season, and one could no longer discern any shrubs or blades of grass in the freshly ploughed fields. The autumn rains had so softened the earth that he sank knee-deep in the furrows, and at every step he found himself in danger of losing a boot. In addition, the dogs, unaccustomed to that kind of hunting, undermined all the hunter's strategies, and the doves had positioned their advanced guard at various points, exactly as an experienced regiment of the old imperial army would have done.

Enraged by this cunning, Baron B. nonetheless continued to harass them with greater fury, although they never once came within his range. He was feeling tired and overcome by thirst, when in a nearby furrow he saw a flourishing raspberry bush laden with ripe fruit.

"How strange!" said the baron. "A raspberry bush in this place . . . and how much fruit! How beautiful and ripe!"

Lowering the hammer of his rifle, he set it next to himself and sat down; then picking the berries one by one from the bush, their purple seeds making them appear prettily silvered with frost, he quenched as best he could the thirst that was beginning to torment him.

He remained seated thus for half an hour, at the end of which he noticed that some singular phenomena were occurring within him.

The sky, horizon, countryside no longer seemed the same to him; it was not that they seemed changed in some fundamental way, but that he no longer saw them with the same feelings as an hour ago. To make use of a more common figure of speech, he no longer saw them with the same eyes.

Among his dogs were several that he felt he had never seen before, and yet as he thought it over more carefully, he recognized them—except that he watched and caressed them all with greater respect than he usually did. Somehow it seemed to him that he was not their owner, and plagued by this doubt, he tried to call them, "Azor, Fido, Aloff!" The dogs who were called approached him readily, wagging their tails.

"Thank goodness," said the baron, "my dogs still seem to be actually my dogs . . . But this sensation I feel in my head, this weight, is peculiar . . . And what are these strange desires I feel, this will I have never had, this species of confusion and doubleness I feel in all my senses? Am I going mad? . . . Let us see, let us reorganize our thoughts . . . Our thoughts?! Yes, of course . . . because I feel as if these ideas are not all mine. Yet . . . reorganizing them is sooner said than done! It is impossible; in other words, I feel something disorganized in my brain . . . I shall be more precise . . . it is organized differently than before . . . there is something superfluous, overflowing, something that aims to make room for itself in my head. It is not harmful, but it nonetheless pushes, knocks very painfully against the walls of my skull . . . I feel as if I am a double man. A double! How strange! And yet . . . yes, there is no doubt . . . at this moment I understand how one can be double.

"I would like to know why these anemone, still sopping wet from the rains, flowers to which I have never in my life paid much attention, now seem to me so beautiful and charming . . . What vivid colors, what a simple and graceful shape! Let us make a nosegay of them."

And the baron, stretching out his hand without rising, gathered three or four of them, which—how singular!—he then put in his breast as women do. But as he removed his hand, he felt an even stranger sensation: he wanted to draw back his hand and at the same time stretch it out again; his arm, seemingly moved by two conflicting but equally powerful wills, remained in that position as if paralyzed.

"My God!" said the baron; and making a violent effort, he came out of that state of rigidity and at once looked closely at his hand as if to see whether something were broken or damaged.

Then he observed, for the first time, how small and shapely his hands were, how long and slender the fingers, how perfect the ellipses described by his nails; and he examined them with unusual satisfaction. He looked at his feet and, seeing that they were small and narrow, notwithstanding the rather clumsy appearance of his boots, he found that he liked them and smiled.

At that moment, a flock of doves rose from a nearby field and were passing in front of him, within shooting range. The baron was quick to stoop down, seize his gun, bend back the hammer, and yet . . . what a prodigious thing! In that instant, he noticed that he was frightened by his own gun, and the roar of the shot would have terrified him. He hesitated and let the weapon fall from his hand, as an inner voice was saying to him, "How beautiful those birds are! What beautiful feathers they have in their wings! . . . They look like wild doves to me . . . "

"Blast it!" exclaimed the baron, raising his hands to his head. "I do not understand a thing about myself anymore . . . Am I still me, or not? Or am I me and someone else at the same time? When have I ever been afraid to fire my rifle? When have I ever had so much compassion for these damned doves that ravage my sown fields? My fields! But . . . truly, they do not seem to belong to me any longer . . . That does it, enough, let us return to the castle; it is probably the effect of some fever that will pass when I jump into bed."

And he made a motion to stand up. At that moment, however, the other will that seemed to exist within him forced him to remain in his initial position, as if it wanted to tell him, "No, let us stay seated a little while longer."

The baron felt that he was gladly assenting to this will when, at a bend in the road flanking the field, a crew of young workers appeared on their way back to the village. He gazed at them with a peculiar feeling of interest and desire that he could not understand. He observed that several of them were quite handsome. When they passed by and greeted him, he responded to their greeting by bowing his head with much embarrassment, and he realized he was blushing like a young girl. Then he felt as if he could rise without any more difficulty, and he stood up. When he got to his feet, he felt lighter than he ordinarily did: at times his legs seemed stiff, at others more limber; his movements were more graceful than usual, although in reality they were the same movements he had always made, and he appeared to be walking, gesturing, swaying as he always had in the past.

He started to sling his rifle across his shoulders but felt that same fear again and decided to carry it on his arm, although kept a little away from his body, as a timid boy would have done.

When he arrived at a point where the road branched off, he was uncertain about which of the two directions he should choose to bring him back to the castle. Both led there, but as a rule he always traveled the same one; now he wanted to take both of them simultaneously. He tried to move but again experienced the same phenomenon he had just gone through: the two wills that seemed to dominate him, working on him with the same forces, were mutually paralyzing, their action rendered useless, and he remained fixed in the road as if petrified, as if struck by catalepsy. After a few moments, he noticed that the state of rigidity abated, his indecision vanished, and he turned to the road he usually traveled.

He had not taken a hundred steps when he encountered the magistrate's wife, who greeted him courteously.

"Since when," wondered Baron B., "have I accustomed to receiving greetings from the magistrate's wife?" Then he recalled that he was Baron B., the signora was an intimate acquaintance of his, and he was amazed that he had asked himself this question.

A little farther on he met an old woman who was rummaging through several bundles of dry branches along the hedge.

"Good day, Caterina," he said, embracing her and kissing her cheeks. "How are you? Have you received any news from your father-in-law?"

"Oh! Your Excellency . . . how gracious you are," exclaimed the old woman, nearly frightened by the baron's unusual familiarity. "I shall tell you—"

But the baron interrupted her, saying, "Please, look at me carefully, tell me: am I still myself? Am I still Baron B.?"

"Oh, sir!" she said.

He did not linger for another reply but proceeded down the road, running his fingers through his hair, exclaiming, "I have gone mad, mad!"

Along the road he stopped often to contemplate objects or people who had never before stirred the slightest interest in him, viewing them from a perspective entirely different from the one he had previously adopted. The beautiful farm girls hoeing in the fields with their skirts hiked up above the knee no longer held any attraction for him: they appeared coarse, untidy, vulgar. Casting a random glance on his bloodhounds walking before him, their noses low, tails dangling, he said, "Look at this! Visir who was only two months old now seems to be over eight; he has even forced his way among the first-rate dogs."

Only a short distance remained before reaching the castle when he met several of his domestic servants walking along the road, chattering away, and—how unusual!—he saw them double: he experienced the same optical phenomenon that occurs when both pupils converge toward the same central point so as to cross the line of vision. He realized, however, that the causes of the phenomenon he was experiencing were in fact different from this optical illusion; he saw double images, but they did not completely resemble one another in their doubleness. He saw them as if he contained two people who looked through the same eyes.

And from that moment on the strange doubleness spread to all his senses; he saw double, heard double, touched double, and—what was even more surprising—he thought double. That is to say, the same sensation provoked in him two ideas, and these two ideas were developed by two different faculties of reason and judged by two different consciences. In a word, he seemed to be living two lives, yet they were conflicting, segregated, by nature different; they could not be fused together, and they struggled in competition for dominance over his senses—hence the doubleness of his sensations.

It was for this reason that when he saw his servants, he certainly recognized them as his servants, but yielding to a stronger impulse, he could not help approaching one of the men, embracing him with transports of delight, and saying to him, "Oh! Dear Francesco, I joy to see you again. How are you? How is our baron?"—and he knew very well that he was the baron—"Tell him he will see me again at the castle before long."

The servants went away, astonished. The one who had been embraced said to himself, "I would rack my brains to know whether or not it was really the baron who spoke to me. I have heard those words before . . . I cannot say . . . but that exclamation . . . that appearance . . . that embrace . . . it certainly wasn't the first time I was embraced like that. And yet . . . my worthy employer has never honored me with so much familiarity."

A few steps farther ahead, Baron B. saw a trellis that rested on one corner of a garden fence, so that when it was covered with leaves, it created a bower inaccessible to the eyes of the curious. He could not repress the desire to enter there, although he was aware of another will that urged him to hasten toward the castle. He yielded to the first impulse, and as soon as he was seated in the bower, he felt himself undergoing a psychological phenomenon that was even more unusual.

A new consciousness was forming in him: the entire canvas of a past he had never known stretched out before his eyes; pure, gentle memories whose growth he could never have nurtured brought a pleasant disturbance to his spirit. There were memories of a first love, and a first sin; but a love more kind and lofty than he had ever felt, and a sin more sweet and generous than he had ever committed. His mind ranged through an unknown world of emotions, traveled through regions never seen, conjured up delights never experienced.

All the same, this ensemble of remembrances, this new existence added to his, was not upsetting and did not confuse memories specific to his own life. An imperceptible line separated the two subjectivities.

Baron B. spent some time in the bower, after which he felt the desire to hasten toward the village. Then, with the two wills working on him in concert, he suffered an impulse so powerful that he could not maintain his usual pace and was forced to break into a headlong dash.

From that instant, the two wills began to control each other and him with equal power. If they worked in concert, his bodily movements were precipitate, convulsive, violent; if one will fell silent, they were normal; if the two wills were opposed, his movements were hindered and gave way to a paralysis that continued until the more powerful one prevailed.

While he was running toward the castle in this fashion, one of his servants saw him, and, fearing some misfortune, called him by name. The baron wanted to stop, but could not; he slowed down his pace and rather paused for a few moments, but this was followed by a paroxysm, a hopping, a fitful advance and withdrawal, so that he seemed possessed and was compelled to continue his dash toward the village.

The village no longer seemed the same to him; he felt as if he had been away for many months. He saw that the campanile of the parish church had recently been repaired, and although he already knew about this change, it still felt as if he had not known.

Along the street he encountered many people who, surprised by his running, stared at him with expressions of amazement. He took off his hat to all of them, although he was aware that this was unnecessary; and they responded by removing their caps, marveling at so much courtesy. But what seemed even more strange was that all those people considered his running and greetings almost natural, and they felt as if they had glimpsed, intuited, grasped something in his actions, but without knowing precisely what it might be. It did, however, make them frightened and concerned.

When he reached the castle, he stopped, entered the anterooms, kissed each of his maids, shook hands with his green-liveried footmen, and threw his arms around the neck of one, whom he caressed with much tenderness as he spoke words of passion and affection.

At this sight, the maids and footmen fled and ran shouting to lock themselves in their rooms.

Then Baron B. climbed to the other floors, visited every room in the castle, and having arrived at his bedchamber, threw himself on his bed and said, "I come to sleep with you, Baron, sir." In that interval of repose, his ideas reorganized themselves; he recalled everything that had happened to him during those two hours, and it terrified him. Yet this was only an instant—very soon he fell back under the domination of that will which directed him as it pleased.

It returned to repeat the words it had said a moment ago: "I come to sleep with you, Baron, sir." And new memories were aroused in his soul; they were double memories—that is, recollections of impressions that the same event leaves in two different spirits—and he welcomed both sorts of impressions in himself. Yet these recollections were not like the ones that had already been evoked under the trellis: those were simple, these complex; those left a part of his soul empty, neutral, impartial; these occupied it totally. And since they were memories of love, at that moment he understood the great unity, the immense inclusiveness of love, which, since the inexorable laws of life make it a sentiment divided in two, can be comprehended only partially by any one person. It was the full and complete fusion of two spirits, a fusion toward which love is only an aspiration, the delights of love no more than a shadow, an echo, a dream of those delights. Nor can I express with less confusion the singular state in which he found himself.

He spent about an hour in this state, after which he noticed that the pleasure was diminishing and the two lives that seemed to animate him were separating. He rose from the bed, passed his hands over his face as if to tear away some light object . . . a veil, a shadow, a feather. Then he felt a different touch; it seemed as if his features had changed, and he experienced the same sensation as if he were caressing another person's face.

There was a mirror nearby, and he ran to gaze in it. How strange! He was no longer himself, or at least he certainly saw his image reflected there, but he saw it as another person's image; he saw two images in one. Through the diaphanous surface of his body shone a second image whose contours were hazy, unstable, familiar. And it seemed very natural to him because he knew that this unity contained two people, that he was not just one person, but two at the same time.

Removing his eyes from the glass, he saw an old, life-size portrait on the opposite wall and said, "Ah! this is Baron B . . . How he has aged!" Then he turned back to study himself in the mirror.

The sight of that painting reminded him that an image hanging in a corridor of the castle resembled the one he had just seen glowing beneath his skin, and he felt overcome by an irrepressible desire to see it again. He rushed toward the corridor.

Several maids walking past at that moment were seized by a fright even more intense than before, and they fled, calling the green-liveried footmen who assembled in the anteroom to plan what has to be done.

Meanwhile, a considerable number of the curious had gathered in the courtyard of the castle: the news of the follies committed by the baron spread through the village in an instant, and the doctor, the magistrate, and other influential people were hurried there.

The decision was made to enter the corridor. The unfortunate baron was found standing before a painting of a young girl— the very girl who had disappeared from the castle some months ago—in a state of nervous excitation impossible to describe. He seemed to be suffering a violent attack of epilepsy; all his vital forces appeared to be riveted on that canvas; he seemed to contain something that wanted to burst out of his body, wanted to break away from it in order to enter the image in the painting. He stared at it apprehensively and took prodigious leaps toward it, as if he were drawn by an irresistible power.

But the most astonishing prodigy was that the longer he stared at the painting, the more his lineaments seemed to metamorphose and acquire a different expression. Everyone recognized him as

Baron B., but at the same time they saw a strange resemblance to the image reproduced in the painting. The crowd packing the corridor halted, stricken by an indescribable panic. What did they see? They did not know; they felt as if they were witnessing some supernatural event.

No one dared draw near—no one moved—an insuperable fear took possession of everyone; a shudder of terror coursed through all their nerves . . .

The baron, meanwhile, continued to hurl himself toward the painting. His excitement mounted, his features were changing more and more, his face reproduced the girl's image with increasing precision . . . and already several people seemed on the verge of bursting into screams of terror, even though a mysterious fear had rendered them mute and motionless. All of a sudden, a voice rose from the crowd, shouting, "Clara! Clara!"

That shout broke the spell. "Yes, Clara! Clara!" the people gathered in the corridor repeated in one voice. Then they began crashing into each other as they rushed for the doors, overwhelmed by an even greater terror. That was the name of the girl who had disappeared from the castle, whose image was reproduced in the painting.

At that shout, Baron B. tore himself away from the painting and dashed into the midst of the crowd, screaming, "My murderer, my murderer!" The crowd scattered and parted. A man fell to the ground in a faint—the very man who had shouted—the young woodsman who had been a suspect in Clara's mysterious disappearance.

Baron B. was forcefully restrained by his green-liveried footmen. The revived woodsman called for the magistrate, to whom he confessed of his own accord that he killed the girl in a jealous rage and buried her in a field, precisely at the spot where a few hours ago he had seen the unfortunate baron sitting and eating the raspberries from the bush.

Baron B. was immediately given a strong dose of an emetic, which made him vomit the undigested fruit and freed him from the girl's spirit.

Her corpse, in whose breast the raspberry bush had taken root, was disinterred and received a Christian burial in the cemetery.

The woodsman was brought to justice and sentenced to twelve years of hard labor.

In 1865, I met him in the penal institution at Cosenza, which he had persuaded me to visit. At that time, two years were remaining in his sentence. It was he himself who told me this marvelous tale.

[1869]

Bouvard

. . . with all deformity's dull, deadly,
Discouraging weight upon me, like a mountain,
In feeling, on my heart as on my shoulders—
An hateful and unsightly molehill to
The eyes of happier man.
BYRON, *The Deformed Transformed*

BOUVARD! Who was Bouvard? Perhaps someone among my readers still attempts—and not without success—to revive in his heart the vague, distant memories annexed to that name; perhaps he yet remembers a mysterious tale that has long stirred youthful reveries of those days and received from all sensitive souls an homage of pity and affection.

I myself strive to recall the circumstances of this piteous story like distant childhood memories, like the fantastic visions of a dream—beautiful and fleeting as they are, harsh and melancholy like everything evocative of sentiment and love.

Nature has destined certain lives for publicity, heaven has

directed that certain intellects be made known to lead the masses like a shining beacon, and nonetheless those lives ended mysteriously neglected, those intelligences wasted away in the shadows, disdainful. Do two forces exist in nature? The positive force that creates and predestines, the negative force that reacts and destroys? Ask the man, ask him the secret of his innermost life, ask the unfortunate genius!

Bouvard was an unfortunate genius. His name faded as rapidly as the precipitate evening star; his life was the transit of a dazzling meteor that burns out in the middle of its arc and disappears in the astonished eyes that marvel at it.

I shall not weave an imagined narrative here: I shall write the story of a man who suffered, the story of a life whose every deed was focused on pain, whose ruin filled with horror and pity every generous soul who knew of it. I write for myself; I write to prolong the memories of my youth throughout my entire life and to preserve for the years of aridity the inexpressible comfort of tears.

Anyone who has never visited the Savoy region—its varied land, its snow-filled valleys, its mountains of pine and granite—is unacquainted with that point on the earth where nature hid the secret of her melancholy. In the Crest-Voland mountains the birds have a sweeter voice, the oriole sings the saddest notes in the hedges, and throughout the territory of the Chablais massif there is a species of wren whose scarcely audible cry resembles a dying man's lament. Along the sides of the mountains, the banks tapestried with white violets (which superstition classes among cemetery flowers) stand out like bright waving ribbons against the dark green of the heather, where swarms of gray butterflies flutter about the dense shrubbery.

Bouvard was born in that place, born in a cabin. His father played the hurdy-gurdy and made a marmot dance in the Champagneux Valley. Bouvard's family made a sad purchase with the birth of this boy: he was stunted and sickly; deformity marked him with its repulsive traces and did not leave anything normal, anything attractive in his face, any charm in his eye or voice. It seems that nature partly repudiated him, allowing him none of the sheer pleasure of life.

When Bouvard was seven years old, he began to notice the derision his deformity earned him, and his heart was pierced, imagining and perhaps foreseeing the fate of his entire existence. His first childhood adversities made him prone to meditation and solitude; and perhaps he owed to this early misfortune the extraordinary development of his sensibility, perhaps even his very genius—because if pain creates or modifies great minds (and in the greatest, misfortune is a cause, not an accident or effect), its action must be more efficacious in the early years of life, when society has still not steeled the heart for protection, and the innocent, virginal spirit retains the indelible marks of nature.

He was forced to part company with his fellows and at night would sit along the banks of the Isère, watching the waters stream by and the sun set behind the forest of Gresy.

"How beautiful the sun is!" Bouvard once said to himself. "How beautiful are these butterflies and these birds that build their nests here! Here is a magnificent lily. How precise in all its parts, how exact in the arrangement of its leaves, how marvelously flexible in its stem!" And in bowing to pick it, he glimpsed his image in the transparent surface of the river—his image, ugly, obscene, hideous . . . Bouvard sat on the bank and wept long, and with abandon. At the very least, he would have liked a heart in which to confide the secret of his early sufferings; and perhaps his mother's melancholy tenderness understood the wealth of emotion enclosed within that boy's delicate soul, perhaps in his mother he found a friend. Yet that friend was soon stolen away from him—at ten Bouvard remained alone in the world.

One day his father told him, "My dear son, you are now ten years old, and although you are somewhat sickly and your appearance is truly not one of the best, your strength is sufficiently developed, and you can henceforth do well enough on your own. I intend to go to France, and it is time for us to part. Take my marmot and my hurdy-gurdy. They are much more than I can give you, but heaven may at least reward your father's generous sacrifice with your success."

Bouvard took the road to Bonneville and slept the first night in a canebrake along the bank of a stream. It was a beautiful night in August. He had never seen so many stars nor heard so clearly the noise of the locusts in the stubble of the harvested fields and the countless soft, indescribable sounds of the leaves on a quiet summer night. Bouvard felt something unusual in himself: he was not asleep, he was not afraid, he felt no weariness, no discomfort, he was calm and peaceful—an infinite feeling of well-being infused every part of his body with a sweetness he had never experienced until then: he was at once thoughtful and serene.

"Listen," he said. "It is a fine thing that this cricket is chirping, but why does it chirp? . . . And what are you doing up there, all those lights God burns every night? . . . And these plants? . . . And this nightingale I hear trilling from afar? I never really noticed that there were so many beautiful things in the sky, or that the crickets sang so sweetly at night. Oh, the Lord must be good if he created so many marvelous things."

Bouvard fell into a deep meditation. He thought of his mother and his cabin and that unknown world he was about to enter so young. Little by little, his senses grew drowsy. He concentrated on the melancholy harmony that soothed his ear like a child's song, the rustling of the stalks, the murmur of the insects, the lament of the water, the voice of the wind and leaves. His soul acquired a strange sensibility, his hearing an ineffable sensory power: he distinguished the most delicate notes, the most melodious tones, the sweetest cadences, and he felt that he perceived the magnificent music of nature. He took his hurdy-gurdy and played an old plaintive air he had once heard from his father. There was nothing more simple than that music, nothing more monotonous than that sound, but he nonetheless found such tenderness in it that his eyes filled with tears, and when he finished, he realized he was kneeling in prayer.

Nature made a momentous revelation to Bouvard in that instant: he understood that he was an artist; through an extraordinary power of intuition, he fathomed the mystery of an entire life. A boundless self-confidence, an irresistible eagerness for the future were then stirring in his heart: he felt proud of himself, proud of his divine art; he was well aware that he had not yet achieved anything, but he knew that everything would be achieved in time.

Bouvard fell asleep because it was very late, and he dreamt of the angels and the flowers, his cabin and his mountains, the white swallows of the Isère and its banks blooming with buttercups . . . He was still dreaming when he felt someone beating on his shoulders, and as he awoke, he saw two men seated near him. One of them, who appeared quite old, was watching him intently.

"My little one," this man said to Bouvard, "it seems to me that you are earning your bread with this ugly marmot and this wretched instrument, and you are still very young to be setting out so alone in the world. I shall give you a companion. Here is my friend Jeanin, from whom I must part this very day. He is a distinguished person and possesses only one small defect, a flaw of no consequence for his art: he is blind in both eyes, but sees perfectly with his mind and has better hearing than us, because my friend Jeanin is not in fact a fool and will bring you decent money with his violin. Truly, your face does not much eulogize your mother, but you seem like a kind boy, and heaven will be obliged to you if you are a good companion to my friend. Come now, untie this tailless marmot's leash immediately, since it will not do well to try your fortune with a badge of poverty, give your hand to your companion, and get going. By noon I must be on the road to Villaz, along the canal."

Bouvard considered this event an extraordinary gift of fortune, and he felt that something agreeable might reside in the mission of charity and love with which heaven seemed to entrust him in his unanticipated alliance to the blind man.

He was not mistaken.

Seven years later, the newspapers in Geneva read: "Bouvard, the celebrated violinist, will give a public performance in our theater this evening. The extraordinary genius of this young artist and the universal fame that precedes him free us from the need to add any words of praise and recommendation."

We next see Bouvard in the second phase of his life—no longer the little Savoyard, but the man of the world, the elegant youth, the extraordinary artist.

What are his passions, his heart?

Lake Leman lies calm and peaceful, the sky is serene and starry, the moon is reflected in the waves. It is one of those nights of silence and love when everything in the creation stirs, alive with this sentiment. What says the whisper of the wind that gently ripples the waters? What say the waters to the wind? Why do the myriad flowers in that tree quiver, whispering among themselves? The dewdrop that descends from the sky to the lodge itself in the flower's cherished calyx—what attractive force showed her the path to him, in the vast universe that created her? Let us attend to this language of beings unappreciated by man. There we hear the drone of the insect performing his nuptials among the scented petals of the rose; the hum of the nocturnal butterfly fluttering around his female companion in her nest of leaves and silk; the voice of the zephyr preparing for the mysterious fecundation of the flowers; the shudder of the seaweed bending to caress the fleeting waves of the stream; the secret language of the stars, the murmuring of the stalks and buds, the fern's kisses, the infinite numbers that reveal in nature the universal and overwhelming sentiment of life—love.

Yet how many men can hear this language? Is not man the only creature to have prostituted love and sacrificed this heavenly sentiment on the altar of his egoism? Do not inquire about love from man, ask him only about a shadow—a hazardous show that feigns, declares, vows . . . There was a time when men loved one another, before the family, that pure, virginal girl, was taken away from the forest and cabins to attend her wedding with society and met gold in her path, the petulant, adventurous boy who did violence to her. From that disgrace egoism was born, the wicked and insatiable monster that devours the emotions to which he himself gives birth, as Saturn once devoured his children.

But just as we sometimes observe, among the hundred withered limbs of a tree blasted by lightning, a single surviving branch dressed in such lovely flowers as that tree never gave forth in the fullness of its youth and spring; not otherwise did love, banished from the womb of humanity, take refuge in the breasts of a few men who preserved it in the secrecy of their hearts. Ask them how to love, what they hope from love, ask them if one can love with impunity. Oh, youth is harsh, and the laws of society are not less harsh! . . . Avoid the struggle, therefore, soil your soul, hurl your crown of roses to the earth before it is torn from your head and replaced by a wreath of thorns and cypress.

An abandoned boat gently rocks on the transparent surface of the lake. The two oars extending from its sides imprint the waves with two parallel furrows of silver, which fill up and form again, without disappearing and without leaving the slightest trace of themselves—fitting emblem of life. For who believes that the future exists? Who believes that the past exists? There is only the present, and it is the imperceptible point that joins them together: time is a chain paid out from the abyss of the future and pulled into the chasm of the past. But perhaps the part that disappears will return—the snake biting its own tail. Who knows whether the past does not resurface with its situations, places, and events? The laws that govern the evolution of stars and worlds—why do they not likewise govern the evolution of time? Everything sets out from a single principle of life: small worlds in a large world, little existences in a great existence . . . Yes, time returns, or else eternity would be no more than the raving of mortals. Can the idea of eternity be conceived where things are dying?

Perhaps these are the ideas stirring in Bouvard's mind as he sits forlorn in his boat. At his young age, he is beginning to experience that malaise of the heart born from deluded hopes and nurtured in solitary affections.

The opening pages of the book of life contain delightful stories, predictions and presentiments of happiness without end, but the pages in the middle prepare for disillusionment, the closing ones for resignation. Often the book is thrown away, and only a few memories of one's reading remain alive. Bouvard did what all unhappy people have done: he devoured the opening pages contemptuously and has now stopped disconsolate in the middle of the book. But he did not read these pages—no, he guessed them; he has not hastened his disillusionment, just anticipated it. In the pleasures of existence he has found only a prostitution unworthy of our nature, a fictitious world that flees us and yet caresses us, a lie that degrades and yet nourishes us . . . Which age in fact is most often the object of nostalgia? Which days do we dare call happy? Youth . . . And yet the period that follows it reveals its errors, strips that seeming, mendacious world of its fatuous and dazzling colors, demonstrates the vanity of those passions, the pettiness of those joys, the nothingness of those pleasures, the ridiculousness of those aspirations, the cruel source of those dreams that promise us the infinite delights of a virile life. Yet if we recognize that fraud to the advantage of truth, how can we dare be nostalgic for it?

Of course, a cruel punishment still weighs on all our heads: wherever the tree of knowledge spreads its branches and entices men to gather forbidden fruits, the terrible sentence heaven hurled down on our fathers seems to be renewed. Every step humanity has so far taken on the road to truth progress has marked a step away from its happiness and moral perfection. What happens to nations happens to the individual; what happens to the existence of the masses happens to private lives. The joys of youth shun those men to whom a precocious intellectual development and fatal habit of reflection have revealed too early the profound nothingness of life and taught that truth is a naked phantom, that our very eagerness to reach it invests it with dazzling colors and celestial shapes, for which only one desperate consolation remains—withdrawal.

Bouvard is only nineteen, and already he has surveyed the tempestuous ocean of existence in its entirety: he perceives glory, fame, prosperity, the noisy, elegant life, all the mild waves that seem to ensure him a calm, secure position. Yet this is not where he wants to rest; he yearns for another shore, distant and unforeseen . . . Dare he name it? Dare he utter it to himself? Bouvard desires love, a love as passionate and infinite as his soul, a love wherewith to satiate himself or die.

He was born to love. There are some lives that are ever but a continuous incessant revelation of this sentiment. Bouvard first loved his mother, and with her his cabin, the flowers and birds of his mountains, then his marmot from which he parted in tears, then his blind companion and the poor villages in the Savoy where they traveled together.

It was above all to his companion that Bouvard directed his piteous cares and affection for many years. That old man had taken the place of a world for him; there he found the harsh tenderness of a father and the confident warmth of a friend. Poor Jeanin was once a well-known artist who, embittered by the malice of the wicked, was later ungratefully forgotten. He wanted to make Bouvard a student destined to vindicate his genius. The youth also followed Jeanin's example by subduing his heart to an infinite tenderness, a sensitivity without comfort, a generosity of soul too great and too often scorned by men. In their peregrinations through the countryside, they sometimes loved to sleep under the open sky on summer nights and breathe in the music of nature. They occasionally went into the villages, but only to let others hear the harmony they derived from it, like a sudden emanation of their genius, like a tribute owed to men who relieved the needs of their material life. Having performed their mission, they returned to the fields, with Bouvard often leading his companion to sit along the riverbanks or in the remote reaches of the valleys, where the wind constantly stirs the broad oak leaves and nightingales sing in the serene nights till morning.

"Do you see the sun?" the old man sometimes asked him. "Is it still as bright as when I saw it in my youth? Give me your hand, let me touch your face and hair; I want to feel whether your features are like mine at that age."

Young as he was, Bouvard slept soundly through the night, and often in his sleep he heard Jeanin talking to himself or praying. One night the old man's sweet playing seemed so sublimely unfamiliar, Bouvard thought that one of the angels, whom he once discussed with his mother, might have descended to teach him a melody that can be heard only in heaven. Then he heard the old man moan and murmur some prayers, then nothing at all. Jeanin was still sleeping when Bouvard awoke in the morning. He waited for his companion to awake and, reluctantly, shook him . . . He was dead! Bouvard wept for several days, then buried him with his violin under three tall trees that grew nearby, along a river that flows into the Rhône: having heard Jeanin say that he was from the village of Montélimar, the youth thought that in time the waters would bear his corpse back to his native land.

At this point, a new future opened before Bouvard's gaze. Although modest, he was aware of his genius; he felt that he was an artist, that he could test himself in places very different from the poor villages in the Savoy. The hope of finding his father, an itinerant puppeteer in France, drew him to that country almost in spite of himself. He entered the Saône region, played for the first time at Bourges, then Mâcon, Moulins, Nevers. Everywhere he won applause, everywhere he provoked the most unexpected admiration. At Melun, the audience threw crowns to him, and since he happened to be so close to Paris, he entered the city, attracted by that noisy, happy life in which he longed to lose himself.

Four years passed. The little Savoyard, the poor hurdy-gurdy player, became an elegant young man, a sought-after artist, the spiritual element of grand gatherings. The social elite competed for Bouvard as if he were the living genius of art or one of those illustrious scientists whose favor and esteem are coveted.

It was in those great towns that he studied men more than they did themselves. He saw clearly that wherever hands stretched out to grasp his, wherever he listened to words of homage, his lips drew near the honeyed poison of adulation. Yet his soul seemed to be offended by that sham existence, and when he sought a heart, just a heart, he realized that a desert opened about him, friendship shunned that seeming, counterfeit life, and his deformity condemned him to be isolated from love.

In every age there are women who sacrifice their reputations to beauty detached from genius—but none who sacrifice themselves to genius detached from beauty. Woman, this quintessence of dust, the most perfect work in the entire creation, often hides the most delicate traces of sensuality behind the irritable mask of modesty. In the passion of love, man is almost always guided by virtue in his choice, woman ever by attractiveness. No woman has solaced the life of some great unfortunate man with a lover's affection. A recent death—the death of the unhappy Leopardi—censures the sensual egoism of woman before the court of humanity.

Bouvard perceived too soon that he could not hope to love, and at the same time he recognized that this need had penetrated his nature so deeply that it could be allayed only by death. Angry with that indifferent, clamorous life where everything is bestowed on appearance, he thought that solitude would put him in greater harmony with himself and realized that he still had something to love—his memories. He was rather well-off; he bid farewell to public life and went traveling through his mountains. But here some unexpected disenchantments were reserved for him: everything was changed in the rustic theater of his childhood. The melting snows had eroded large portions of the cliffs at various points; the mountaineers had felled a favorite pine forest where he used to rest in the dog days of August; all that remained of his cabin was a heap of rocks where green lizards flashed in the sunlight. As he came to his friend's grave, he found that the loose, damp soil was completely covered with that vermillion cyclamen which grows in the mountains, and he picked a bit of it to carry with him for the rest of his life, the only relic that had survived the shipwreck of his happiness and youth.

That grave was the site whereon he composed the most beautiful melodies the genius of music could ever inspire, as a tribute to the holy memory owed to the man who had taught him the rudiments of art and revealed the most sublime mysteries of harmony.

But as no one is capable of remaining unhappy long, Bouvard thought that a sojourn in a large city would divert him from his disconsolate meditations, and his pain was nearly dulled and soothed. The fame of *La Nouvelle Héloïse*—the most beautiful book ever written about love—was still widespread and flourishing among the passionate youth of that era. Bouvard devoured its pages in a kind of delirious fever. The great socialist's life was then declining, splendid and majestic as one of those stars that blaze more brightly before they vanish from men's sight. Bouvard wanted to kiss the soil that had given life to Jean-Jacques, and he went to Geneva.

Here we see him again in that city, in the silence of a starry night, alone, forsaken on a boat in the middle of the tranquil waves of Lake Leman. What is he doing? What is the young man thinking at that moment?

There are periods of excitement in the growth of the human spirit, when the soul is sublimed and elevated to an immeasurable grandeur inconceivable to anyone but itself. What word dares display those impulses? The word can express only small passions, the sensations inherent in matter. Yet everyone possesses something that he does not reveal, that he cannot reveal; everyone is greater than what he appears to be, than what perhaps he himself believes he is. And what do we call genius, if not the faculty of imagining and expressing, with as much truth as possible, this profoundly secret spiritual life of man?

Bouvard gazes at the stars, the sky, the motionless surface of the lake, the willows bending over the banks, the fish darting after one another, the fireflies sparkling in the oar-stirred waves. And from this varied spectacle he derives ideas that he feels, understands, but is still unable to articulate to himself. It is the arcane language between us and nature that God has not permitted man to voice.

But the young man's eyes insistently turn to the distant lights that appear on the banks like so many motionless sentries in the night, to the villas scattered along to the shore, to their windows, half-closed and lit, hiding countless mysteries of happiness and love. Beneath each of those roofs lives a family, hearts loving one another, hopeful and joyous, whose existence is not entirely woven with pain . . . To feel oneself born to love, to possess a heart capable of loving a universe, and yet to search the desert of life in vain for some answer to the incessant call of the spirit—always in vain! Eternally in vain! "Beauty, cruel beauty! Why was the absolute empire of love granted to you alone? Why are you the only revelation, the sole sensible form of this sentiment? Why?" exclaims Bouvard. "Why imprison my soul in a creation so abhorrent to nature? Why give me this Ethiope's profile, this Hottentot's nose, this Laplander's mouth? Could deformity dress me in more repulsive clothing? The terrible sentence that joins visible ugliness with moral beauty and destines the one to reveal the other!"

After that night Bouvard fell ill. He had barely recovered when he abruptly left Geneva and traveled into Italy.

Three years passed. He went to Venice, Rome, Florence, and finally stopped at Naples where, rich in fame and money, he resolved to end his artistic career in mystery and isolation.

The most extreme and unanticipated disillusion struck him in those last years of his triumph: he disdained his art. Why should he use it to create an ideal, fantastic world that society refused to let him attain? Why caress his illusions, palliate his misfortune, excite his sensibility, if he already noted the vanity of these remedies and if his pride insistently ordered him to shun them? Why squander his treasures of harmony, the superabundance of his art, on a thoughtless throng who showered him with gold, acclaimed him a divine artist, but whom he would have begged in vain for even one of those emotions he aroused so powerfully in their hearts? They admired the artist in him, not the man, his genius, not the delicate feeling that accompanied it, not the ineffable martyrdom that paid for it. He felt beaten, gripped by a depression he would have pointlessly tried to overcome. To live for himself and by himself, to forget, even to hate, perhaps even hate, since hate can very well deny his desire for love—this is Bouvard's ultimate resolution, the desperate comfort he expected from his plan.

He then withdrew to a remote villa near Posillipo and lived for an extended period in obscurity. Perhaps oblivion would have erased his name forever from the pages of fame, if a mysterious event had not inscribed it with indelible characters, if a terrible catastrophe had not illuminated his premature decline with a dismal, frightening light.

Bouvard was twenty-five years old, and he had not loved. Rather, he desired love—longed for a woman's affection as one longs for the ideal affect of an angel—he begged heaven for it like a madman. For a brief, fleeting moment of love, he would have accepted an entire lifetime of agony. At twenty-five, love is no longer a vague aspiration, no longer the changeable, indecisive, extremely unfocused sentiment that develops in youth, but a novel feeling that is transmitted throughout our being and gathers all the spiritual and physical threads of our existence. The life granted to men lies in the exact harmony of spirit and matter, and true, powerful love balances them evenly; every affection that evades these laws is opposed to the laws of nature. It is at twenty-five that woman is loved; at fifteen, only love itself.

Yet if Bouvard's soul was delicate and sensitive, at the same time it was also severe. If he was unable to ignore his own deformity, he did not fail to appreciate the loftiness of his spirit and mind: a common affection was not worthy of him; he would rather pine away in the awful solitude of his passions than accept the love of a woman who could not understand the treasures of poetry and emotion concealed in his lacerated heart.

To the lover's gaze, virtue is revealed only in beauty. Beauty and goodness seem to share the same nature, to couple and display one another—it could be said that goodness is moral beauty, and beauty visible goodness. Bouvard deceived himself, as all men do: he did not realize that an inexplicable force often keeps them separate, nor that this fatal contradiction emerges distinctly and more often than not in the vacuous nature of woman. No matter how seldom one has lived in society or drawn lessons from experience, it will be observed that the fabled beauties of every period are distinguished by a moral defect, often by a wicked heart or unbridled vice; it is the mediocre beauties who figure among the women with the best and sweetest dispositions, perhaps because their number is more widespread. Yet deformity exceeds these bounds and almost always shows signs of extreme goodness or wickedness. Bouvard, wanting to seek out virtue, sought beauty and found it.

One autumn evening, as he sat along the seashore in one of those delightful little inlets formed here and there by the water's erosion of the surrounding rocks, he was contemplating the sunset behind the serrated reefs of Lacco Ameno, when a boat suddenly passed near the beach. An elderly lady sat in the prow reading, and not very far from her a most beautiful young woman meditated in silence, her eyes lifted toward the sky in an attitude of rapturous abandon, a hand dangling deathlike from the side of the boat, the palest fingers grazing the waves that encircled her like a moving bracelet of pearls and silver. A pure white sail swelling with wind, the celestial light of the sunset mirrored in the waves, the waves crashing on the shore composed the background of that marvelous painting, which slipped by and vanished before the young man's eyes like an instantaneous creation of his fancy or the heavenly vision of a dream. The woman had not so much seen Bouvard as beheld him—beheld him at length. Her motionless, staring eyes seemed to pour into him sentiments that perhaps sprang from the thought of a distant, beloved creature, and he seemed to be made the object of aspirations that were heavenly in origin and that the maiden would have tried in vain to reveal on earth.

Bouvard knew that he could not be loved, but his faith in woman's sacrifice was still so great that he believed he could be loved out of compassion. He felt that he possessed an enticement—misfortune—and he ascribed to it the omnipotence of beauty. No, it is not true that love inspired by compassion can breed humiliation in whomever receives it; such love is the most proud, most noble, and most durable of the passions, perhaps the only one that heaven blesses and that dies with life alone, because only with the passing of life does the misfortune that bred it pass away.

Bouvard attributed that gaze to himself. "She loves me," he said. "She has divined my suffering. And could that angelic face counterfeit a sentiment that was not pity and tenderness? Could she love a happy man? . . . Insolent, jesting, mendacious happiness!" He had seen the woman on other occasions, seen her in his dreams, every night, for seventeen years: she was the fantastic genius of his art, the severe creation of his music, the concretized being, alive, sensitive, vibrant, whom he had composed in the ecstasy of his melodies and meditations.

Indeed, each one of us, from the first years of life, creates the ideal woman he would like to love; each of us believes in the existence of a sisterly spirit, whose features and aspirations are well known to us and for whom we feel an attraction, in spite of ourselves, throughout our lives. The love that consumes itself restlessly is nothing more than the unknown attraction for a creature whom distance, society, and fortune deny us; and often we wander from love to love without reaching her, always anxious and always unsatisfied, lovers always but without ever loving, carrying to the grave the tremendous void that a thousand fleeting affections were powerless to fill.

When Bouvard became aware of his passion, it felt like dismay, like pleasure mixed with pain, like a new intuition of life joined to the vague presentiment of misfortune that heaven had destined for him with that emotion. The lady vanished—would he see her again? Where? When? If he saw her again, would she remember him? Would she love him? Would that interval of time alter the sentiment of pity and love that the young man believed he had read in her eyes?

The instant when love is first revealed to a soul is the most solemn moment in life. What kind of man is he who is capable of forgetting it? No matter how numerous our passions may be, no matter how unworthy of us, no one can ever forget the moment of his first experience of love. It is the revelation of this sentiment that signals the beginning of every man's moral life.

We shall not allude to the changes that occurred in Bouvard's habits and character after that day. He passed three months without seeing her again. He ran up and down every street in Naples like a madman, went to every theater, frequented every gathering place without discovering any sign of her, almost relinquishing the hope of finding her—until one morning he saw her in an elegant carriage crossing Via di Chiaja, heading toward the villa. Bouvard had no time to mull over the most suitable plan that would enable him to overtake her; drawn by an irresistible force, he dashed after the carriage . . . then grew tired . . . but endured . . . stayed even with it for a long time, yet already his zeal was diminishing, his strength abandoned him, and he stopped, exhausted, in the middle of the street. Another month passed: he saw her a second time, with the same outcome; he saw her a third time and, alas, still in vain. But his exertions were finally rewarded: one day he succeeded in following her home. At last he knew her abode, her nest, that envied point on the earth where an adored woman lives . . . What joy! He dared to inquire about her: her name is Giulia, she is only seventeen, a girl, wealthy, happy, with a heart pure as her soul, free as the light that encircles her.

From that day onward, Bouvard grew bold: he ventured to hope that he was loved, ventured to think of revealing his passion and of hastening the opportunity to do it with the prestige of his art and fame. It did not take him long to overcome the obstacles that denied his approach to her, and at length, the moment he so ardently yearned for arrived, the moment when he could be intoxicated with her sight and confidently read the unknown pages of his destiny.

Giulia belonged to a patrician family, around whom the flower of the aristocracy and the most celebrated names in the arts and sciences would gather. It was to one of these artistic soirées that Bouvard received an invitation; he was joyfully welcomed there, heard with transport, applauded with frenetic enthusiasm . . . But oh, God! Was this the same Giulia he had first seen from the shore at the melancholy moment of sunset? . . . That girl, so beautiful, sweet, compassionate, that gentle, thoughtful being who appeared to him like a heavenly vision in the awful hour of his misery? She, that angel, his beloved, was nothing but an ordinary woman, happy, carefree, having a gay time, smiling at all those fatuous, elegant people who competed for her affection—a creature of society and pleasure, rich in youth and beauty, self-confident because happy, and happy because too insensible, too immune to that infirmity of mind and heart which renders us sympathetic to every social ill, wherever it may be, and compels us to share it.

Perhaps Bouvard was not wrong in thinking that the girl recognized him and laughed at his affection and deformity. Giulia's demeanor contained too much derision and indifference, so that he could at least flatter himself for not betraying his secret . . . that secret, so sweet, so dear, cherished so long, whose revelation now oppressed him with shame and humiliation. And the fact was that the young man who had followed her carriage like a fool, who had prostituted his dignity and his pride, who had laid claim to her heart in such a strange guise and with such a strange insistence, was now speechless, mortified, tacitly mocked . . . Besides, what was he to her? . . . He . . . that artist, virtually ignored because he disdained admiration, that poor Savoyard, that timid, suffering, misshapen young man?

Bouvard understood too late that a fatal blindness had flattered him with an affection that his deformity rendered him incapable of inspiring. His deformity . . . that alone, always that . . . the inexorable sentence, the terrible distinction, the indelible mark of nature, which neither art, nor emotion, nor genius had the power to destroy. A horrible desire then flashed through his mind—the desire for a more monstrous deformity, an ugliness so frightening that by driving men to shrink from it, he could satiate his inexpressible greed for hate, the nascent greed that was already supplanting the first, noble aspiration of love in his soul.

Such are the vicissitudes of the affections. Often, it is only the temperate, ordinary ones that fade into apathy. No middle course is permitted the great passions, however, and hate and love, which mark their two highest points, alternate at the apex of their power without admixture or cessation. Which of these two passions is the most noble and just is still unresolved, since one comes from heaven, the other from earth, one prevails in society, the other in private life. But it is quite certain that in the majority of men hate alone ultimately fills the void that love cannot fill.

We shall not say that Bouvard hated: events in his later life are not so clear as to enable the confident assertion that he did. Perhaps he only desired hate—that the good always desire in vain to become wicked, and the wicked good, is a distressing aspect of our nature. Does innate goodness kill hate, then? And what is this fatal predestination that our will is powerless to destroy?

Bouvard still loved Giulia—because of a strange contradiction in the human spirit, because of the irresistible potency that beauty exercised over him, he still loved the girl. But she was no longer the ideal Giulia, the creature of his dreams, celestial, reflective, loving; he loved a woman, a woman who was alive, gay, sensual, the quivering image of joy and pleasure. Why should he hate her? By what right did he dare claim the sacrifice of her beauty and heart? If the idea of such a sacrifice, if the noble, disinterested sentiment of love, if affection isolated from matter can be conceived on earth, these feelings are not in the least earthly, yet often the revelation of this truth casts forever into the mud the delicate, sensitive souls that once believed it.

After that day Bouvard's life was wrapped in a mystery so inscrutable that we are unable to refer, not even hypothetically, to the changes which occurred in his spirit and heart. It was only the last instant of his existence that cast an uncertain, sinister light on his past and somehow tied together the broken and scattered threads of his destiny. Where he lived and in what manner, whether exultant or not, remain unknown. He disappeared at the height of his youth and glory. His residence was found deserted, his mirrors shattered, every object that could reflect his image in his eyes was destroyed; every trace he left of himself acknowledged his mental excitement as well as some inflexible, desperate purpose.

We shall not see him again until the last day of his life.

Four years after the last incident—on a fragrant May morning, during the season that invites nature to love—the doors of a sumptuous palace were decked in mourning . . . Giulia, the wealthy, noble, elegant patrician, was dead—dead on the eve of her nuptials, snatched from the earth by a cruel and sudden illness, in all the fullness of her illusions and faith, in all the vigor of her youth and beauty.

At that moment, the small window in the attic of the opposite house showed the figure of a man whose pain-altered lineaments were twisted into a terribly bitter smile. It was Bouvard. The sepulchral pallor of his face, the unkempt growth of his hair and beard, the lucid, motionless stare, the gloomy, indefinable expression that misfortune had cast over his features like a funeral veil, all betrayed the secret of the profound, supernatural suffering that interweaves many lives in this world, always shunning familiarity and publicity, proud and disdainful of any humiliating compassion, any impossible comfort. And in fact whatever he suffered has always remained a mystery. Did he still love Giulia? Had he not forgotten her in that four-year separation? Did he always live near her? It is certain that he was her neighbor for only four months, during which the most crushing poverty often came to visit his humble artist's garret.

Bouvard looked, saw, read the funeral inscription, observed the black cloth that adorned the deceased girl's doors, observed it with a mute indifference, without grief, without amazement; it could be said that this misfortune did not seem unexpected to him, that he had foreseen, invoked, hastened it, perhaps with desire. Of course, the wicked genius that had provoked men to tell fantastic tales about him would no longer smile sadly, would never show a more evil or cruel satisfaction. The young man shut the window, obsessed with an insistent thought, an idea that was fixed, comforting, long cherished. "Let us hurry," he said, "let us hurry the moment I yearned for . . . let us prepare for my wedding"—and an instant later, the remaining furnishings of the attic, his books, his music, the residue of his fortune had disappeared. Bouvard changed them into gold and used it all to purchase flowers.

The season was fertile. The infinite family of hyacinths, flowers of youth and spring, the first roses, symbol of nascent love, the orange blossoms that weave the crowns of the betrothed, jasmine's shooting stars symbolizing demure love, lavender signifying bold love, azaleas and gardenias, flowers of passion and sentiment—all adorned the modest garret in such great quantities and with such dense fragrance that it could have been taken for one of those fabled dwellings where the fairies enticed bold, heedless youth to marry, destined to perish in an intoxication of pleasure and perfume.

Bouvard attended to this strange transformation of his room

with irrepressible joy: he wanted to know the language of each flower, wanted to arrange them himself, alternating them with pink and blue veils and adding, with a sad smile, several stems of rosemary in bloom, which signifies reciprocal love. Hundreds of lamps were arranged to pour torrents of light on the veils and the thick carpets of flowers; and since the young man carried out his preparations with the most painstaking mystery, he rejoiced at that delightfully alluring sight and said to himself, enraptured, "Now both my bridal chamber and my grave are in readiness . . . life and death . . . the chill of the tomb and the fire of a long-repressed love . . . Certainly, a match more worthy of human beings was never made on earth. Divinity itself might well envy my wedding."

We ask with hesitation: was Bouvard guilty? Had not pain already distorted his reason? Could the soul that was once so pure, so innocent, so generous be so wretchedly transformed? Could it conceive such a horrible plan in the full light of its potency? We cannot answer in the affirmative. Surely, his nature underwent a grievous alteration: poverty, disillusionment, social skepticism, isolation no doubt provoked in him that revolt which leads us to react against the deity and ourselves. Yet his guilt was only the consequence of a sudden confusion of his reason. His crime was expiated by his life, and the expiation preceded it. There was love in this crime, and I would even add genius—the epochs of human existence have few pages so sublime, and our passions are seldom elevated to a more immense power. It could be said that Bouvard's last day was the recapitulation of his entire life.

The nights in southern Italy possess a soft, voluptuous quality: the sky is higher, the blue more transparent, the stars more numerous and brighter. The flowers of the frail magnolia and orange trees open twice annually, suffusing the air with their delicate scents, full of something other flowers do not have—the feeling of love, the breath of youth and abandon. I have asked myself many times why heaven destined those hours for repose. But perhaps night is the calmest and most marvelous scene of nature only because it is at night that men love. The sublime epic of the night! I would like to know whether the dead still retain a portion of their spiritual life on their stone beds, whether that dust—since it exists—is conscious of existing. In the pitch darkness that cloaks all the secrets of nature, I believe that no one can smile at this thought: superstition still has its claims, since it is always its shadows that send forth the first glimmers of truth and light. But have you ever spent a night in a cemetery? The silence there is more forbidding than at any other point on the earth, but you nevertheless have the heightened sense that something is living, thinking, stirring beneath you. Of course, if the dead live, it must be a life of solemn meditation . . . And how do you pass those long winter nights? . . . The infinite years of their mute existence? . . . In the rain, sun, snow . . . Poor souls! No, it is not true that death equalizes all destinies; the wealthy have constructed mausoleums, where they still maintain a ray of that light for which they were so greedy in life.

In one of those most splendid dwellings Giulia's corpse is placed, and the young woman rests in her shroud as if wrapped in the veils of her virginal bed. Her beauty has lost none of its seductiveness. A white dress, light, almost diaphanous, covers her modest figure; her black hair is unbound and drawn back from her brow by a crown of still fresh tuberose flowers. Her pure white hands lie at her sides with the gentle surrender of sleep, and only her feet, pointing upward and joined together, bear witness to the horrible rigidity of death.

Bouvard enters the tomb with joy engraved on his countenance, with that breathless but sweet trepidation which accompanies the first sinful tryst with a desired woman. The horror does not hold him back, does not bridle his impatience, does not diminish the irresistible eagerness of his passion. Every delay can be fatal to his design—he must hasten its execution—his gold has procured him accomplices . . . He steals the girl's corpse, and within a few moments he is alone with her in his secret, solitary abode.

The young man sweetly hays her on a mass of flowers, then kneels down and stares at her . . . The pure white gown, the long, unbound tresses, the limp body nearly sunk in the immobility of death on a verdure-scented bed, the dazzling light painting every object in shades of gold and topaz form a strange spectacle, exalting and ravishing Bouvard's imaginative mind. But he still has not dared to lift the veil concealing her face: he trembles at those features, fears that death has already altered her beauty, fears that fixed, severe gaze whose terrible stillness must taunt him with his crime. A thousand thoughts are now stirring in his troubled soul, the thought of his suffering, his futile love, his unhappy genius, the self-abandonment that dragged him from one day to the next, always hesitating, always disheartened to the point of ending his life in crime—since he feels the nearness of his end, has irrevocably decided to die . . . to die near her, near the woman at whose side he could not spend the fortunate, innocent life that had once been his dream.

With this allusion he is confronted by all the memories of his early youth, those trustful, happy years when the eagerness for the unknown painted the future scenes of his life in a thousand lovely colors: the illusions, the dreams, that bold, unfailing faith, fortune's courteous smile, the universal love whose desire is to strew roses on every man's head, that yearning for a home and family, for perpetuating our existence in other creatures born from us, planning the good and achieving it, fixing it beforehand as the only goal of life . . . What falsehood and cruelty lie in those aspirations! He has nothing left: he suffered, and he continues to suffer; this is everything, this is the synthesis of his hopes—he kneels before a corpse, and the last of his days is about to end in crime. Bouvard is shaken and weeps. In that period of spiritual tranquility preceding death, our intellect enjoys a moment of extraordinary lucidity, during which the entire somber canvas of our past unfolds before our eyes. Joy, pain, affection, guilt—it all passes before us again, all evoked by the inexorable conscience. Happy are those whose gentle, comforting memories leave nothing to regret in life!

Bouvard turns his gaze over his past and perceives only a limitless desert, a barren land without oases, water, greenery, lacking heaven's smile. Twenty-nine years have passed, and he has not gathered a single one of those flowers that nature lavishes on all men. From the tree of life he has plucked only one fruit, a bitter, poisonous fruit, the cruelest of those that mature on its branches—the fruit of derision.

At this thought, the young man's mind, lost in the abyss of his memories, suddenly returns to himself, to his deformity, to Giulia: he observes the lovely, inanimate body that lies before him—that creature desired so long—that girl who was once so beautiful, so gay, so carefree, whose love would have consumed him in the luxuriance of his happiness, whose hate has helped him survive her through an obstinate potency of will.

Whence proceeds that incomprehensible alarm which seizes us

in front of a cadaver? What is this pointless, hypocritical respect that draws us, silent and humble, to a heap of scattering dust? Oh, the shameless impudence that bends men's knees before the remains of a creature whose happiness was violated occasionally, whose life was poisoned countless times!

But such is not Bouvard's situation: he alone has suffered, he alone is the victim. He would like to stand over her as a judge, yet an inner conviction tells him that the years do not gauge existence, only happiness, the single, irrevocable happiness he lost—that girl is dead, but she was happy; he lives, but suffers. He survives her only to remember it.

This thought cruelly upsets the young man's soul, plunging him back into his plans for revenge: the cadaver now seems menacing to him. Perhaps it sees, hears, smiles, stirs beneath its shroud . . . Bouvard rises impulsively and tears away the veil that covers the girl's face. —God! What irresistible beauty! Can the face of a corpse be so beautiful? An expression of heavenly calm spreads over her features, her cheeks are still slightly pink; the pure white forehead, the half-closed lips and eyes, the fair, transparent skin: there is nothing frightening in her, nothing in life could be more graceful, more sweet, more attractive . . . She rests—sleeps—as girls sleep at seven years old, when they dream only of clouds, butterflies, angels . . . things constantly aloft, journeying toward heaven.

Life contains only two momentous events capable of suffusing our faces with a ray of the celestial beauty that eludes manifestation: love and death—two sisters—the ecstasy of the one, the tranquility that follows the other. Those who have and were loved know: the beauty to which I refer is not of the earth and does not endure; it is something airy that alights on our features of a moment and vanishes—it can be seen, but it is inexplicable—it is perhaps a light from above which descends to bless the two most solemn acts in life, the love that renders us worthy of heaven, the death that allows us to reach it.

I have often thought that if all men fell in love at the same time, society would be transformed instantaneously: the golden age would no longer be that charming fable which provokes laughter, like a child's dreams. Every man who loves is good and noble. Poets are lovers.

Bouvard halts at that sight, overcome by enthusiasm: the spell of that beauty ravishes him, exciting his passionate mind and his fervid imagination. His violent gesture bared part of the girl's breast: she appears to him like a toppled statue by Phidias, like one of those images of Greek virgins torn from their base by a storm and sometimes encountered half-buried among the corymbs and the dark ivy leaves on the solitary islands of the Aegean. Divine beauty!—Why was he not empowered to revive her? To inspire her with the breath of life that God has reserved for himself alone?

But Giulia would hate him if she were alive—had she not mocked him?

The young man remains silent a long time. Then his countenance assumes a grim, resolute expression, and he bends over her, wanting to embrace her . . . "No woman," he says, "ever gave herself with greater abandon to a man . . ." Bouvard smiles at this horrible thought, bows his head, and kisses her death-stiffened lips. Her touch! He shudders, starts back in horror, shivers at that intense cold and falls prostrate before the girl. Then he weeps, entreats, prays. He wants to love her, to adore her like a saint, but the memory of his past checks him; he wants to loathe her, but that sweet angelic image arrests him. Several moments later, he is talking wildly, raving, shouting his beloved Giulia's name over and over again, surrendering himself to his desperate, savage pain. The asphyxiating odor of the flowers gradually subdues his senses, intoxicates and confounds his reason: his head is spinning, he sees objects moving, hears the whisper of incomprehensible voices, strange figures pace back and forth before his eyes, watching him, sneering . . . He is agitated, wants to hurl himself against them, attempts to stand again, groping in the void, and falls back down near the girl's corpse, exhausted . . .

But Bouvard did not meet a death so sudden or so violent; in the morning, the neighbors reported hearing moans and muffled screams deep into the night. Yet what most struck their imaginations was the sound of a violin, which enchanted and seduced them as if it were a supernatural harmony. And they have never been persuaded, no matter what evidence was put before them, that the music was the work of a man.

Such was Bouvard's final creation, his soul's final lament, the sublime agony of his genius. It contained all the voices of nature, the whisper of the wind and the fluttering of the birds, the rustling of the slender stalks and the roar of the huge oak boughs, the rush of the rivulet and the crash of the ocean's waves—it contained every sound, harsh and sweet, gentle and horrible. Yet how unfortunate are the people who heard that music! For them, the voice of the dearest creatures, the name of the father uttered for the first time by the child's lips, the first revelation of love to an adored woman have forever lost their gentleness and charm.

The next day, the news of the violated grave spread through the city, and a search was conducted for Giulia's corpse. The clues left by Bouvard's accomplices led to his garret. He was called; no one answered. His door was beaten; no one opened it. Then it was knocked down . . . What a ghastly sight! All the flowers were trampled and scattered, many objects were smashed, the girl's veils torn, everywhere the traces of a desperate, unequal struggle.

Had not Giulia died? Or did the young man's prayers have the power to revive her for an instant? . . .

Splinters and fragments of a violin lay strewn across the floor, and a deformed, inanimate body was locked in a convulsed embrace with the beautiful Giulia's corpse . . . Bouvard was dead!

[1867]

A Dead Man's Bone

I LEAVE TO MY reader the task of assessing the inexplicable incident I am about to relate.

In 1855, having taken up residence at Pavia, I devoted myself to the study of drawing at a private school in that city, and several months into my sojourn, I developed a close friendship with a certain Federico M., a professor of pathology and clinical medicine who taught at the university and died of severe apoplexy a few months after I became acquainted with him. He was very fond of the sciences and of his own in particular—he was gifted with extraordinary mental powers—except that, like all anatomists and doctors generally, he was profoundly and incurably skeptical. He was so by conviction, nor could I ever induce him to accept my beliefs, no matter how much I endeavored in the impassioned, heated discussions we had every day on this point. Nevertheless—and it pleases me to do this justice to his memory—he had always shown himself tolerant of convictions he did not hold, and I and all his acquaintances have cherished the dearest remembrance of him. A few days before his death, he had persuaded me to attend his lectures on anatomy, adducing that I would derive from them not a little knowledge beneficial to my art. I consented, although with repugnance; and goaded by vanity to appear less frightened than I was, I asked him for several human bones, which he gave me and which I placed on the mantel of the fireplace in my room. At his death I ceased frequenting the anatomy course; later I discontinued my study of drawing as well. Nonetheless, I kept the bones for many years, so that the habit of seeing them made me almost indifferent. No more than a few months have passed since, seized by sudden fears, I resolved to bury them, keeping only a simple kneecap. From the first moment I possessed it, I had destined this smooth, spherical bone, because of its shape and smallness, to fill the office of a paperweight, since it alone did not conjure up any frightening ideas in me, and it had already rested on my desk for eleven years when I was deprived of it in an inexplicable way I am about to relate.

In Milan last spring, I met a hypnotist who is well known among lovers of spiritualism, and I requested to be admitted to one of his séances. A little later I received an invitation to attend one, and I went, troubled by such grim suspicions that many times along the way I was almost on the point of turning back. The insistence of my amour propre spurred me on, in spite of myself. I shall not pause here to discuss the astonishing invocations I witnessed; suffice it to say that I was so amazed at the responses we heard from several spirits, and my mind was so struck by those prodigies, that overcoming every fear, I felt the desire to summon a person of my own acquaintance and address to him several questions which I had already pondered and debated in my mind. After revealing this desire, I was brought to a secluded study where I was left alone. The impatience and desire to invoke many spirits at once rendered me irresolute regarding the choice, but since it was my design to interrogate the invoked spirit on human destiny and the spirituality of our nature, I remembered Dr. Federico M., with whom, when he was alive, I had had some fascinating discussions on these topics, and I decided to summon him. Having made his choice, I seated myself at a desk, arranged a sheet of paper before me, dipped the pen in ink, settled myself in a writing posture, and concentrating for as long as possible on that thought, gathering all my willpower and directing it to that end, I waited for the doctor's spirit to arrive.

I did not wait long. After several minutes' delay I noticed, from new and inexplicable sensations, that I was no longer alone in the room; I heard his presence, so to spea, and before I could regain sufficient composure to formulate a question, my shaken, convulsed hand, moved as by a force external to my will, wrote these words of which I had no prior knowledge:

*They are addressed to you. You have called me at a moment
when the most exacting invocations prevent me from coming;
I can neither remain here now nor respond to the questions
you intended to ask me. Nevertheless, I have obeyed your
summons to please you, and because I myself am in need of
you; I have long sought the means to communicate with your
spirit. During my mortal life, I gave you several bones which I
removed from the dissecting room in Pavia; among them was a
kneecap that belonged to the body of a former employee of the
university whose name was Pietro Mariani and whose corpse
I chose at random to dissect. For eleven years now, he has
tortured my spirit to recover the inconsequential little bone, and
he continues to reproach me bitterly for that act, threatening
me and insisting on the restitution of his kneecap. I implore
you, by the perhaps not unpleasant memory you may cherish
of me, if you still have the bone, return it to him, redeem me
from this tormenting debt. I shall send Mariani's spirit to you
immediately. Respond.*

Terrified by that revelation, I answered that I had the unfortunate kneecap, I would be happy to restore it to its rightful
owner, and since there was no other way to make the restitution,
he should send Mariani to me. Having said that—or, more accurately, having thought it—I felt as if my person were unburdened,

my arm freer, my hand no longer numbed as it had been a short while ago, and I realized, in a word, that the doctor's spirit had departed.

Then I sat waiting another moment—my mind was in a state of exaltation impossible to describe.

In the space of a few minutes, I again experienced the same phenomena as before, although with less intensity; and my hand, drawn by the spirit's will, wrote these words:

> The spirit of Pietro Mariani, former employee of the University of Pavia, is before you, and he demands the kneecap of his left knee which you have wrongfully held for eleven years. Respond.

This language was more concise and forceful than that of the doctor. I replied to the spirit: "I am most willing to return to Pietro Mariani the kneecap of his left knee, and I beg him, in fact, to forgive me for the unlawful possession; I desire to know, however, how I can effect the restitution that is demanded of me."

Then my hand started to write again:

> Pietro Mariani, former employee of the University of Pavia, will come himself to recover his kneecap.

"When?" I asked, terrified.

And my hand instantly scrawled a single word:

Tonight.

Stupefied by that response, covered with a cadaverous sweat, I hastened to exclaim, immediately changing the tone of my voice: "Please . . . I beg you . . . do not trouble yourself . . . I will send— there are other less bothersome means—" But I had not finished the sentence when I noticed, from the return of the sensations I experienced initially, that Mariani's spirit had already withdrawn, and there was no longer any way to prevent his coming.

It is impossible for me to express verbally the anguish I was suffering at that moment. I was prey to a dreadful panic. I left that house as the clocks of the city were striking midnight; the streets were deserted, there were no lights in the windows, the flames in the street lamps were dimmed by a thick, heavy fog—everything seemed to me more sinister than usual. I walked for a piece without knowing where to direct my steps: an instinct more powerful than my will drove me away from my house. Where would I find the mettle to go there? That night I would receive a visit from a ghost—it was a ghastly idea, an expectation too terrible to bear.

Wandering down some strange street, as chance would have it,

I found myself in front of a tavern where I saw the words "Domestic Wines" cut into a window hanging illuminated by an interior light, and presently I said to myself, "Let me go in here, this way is better, and it is not a cowardly remedy; I shall seek in wine that boldness which I no longer have the power to ask of my reason." And having ensconced myself in a corner of a huge cellar room, I called for a few bottles of wine, which I drank greedily, although as a rule I am disgusted by any abuse of that liquor. I obtained the effect I desired. At every glass I drank, my fear vanished appreciably, my thoughts grew lucid, my ideas seemed to reorganize themselves, albeit into a new disorder; and little by little I won back my courage to such a degree that I laughed at my terror, stood up, and resolutely set out for my house.

Having reached the room, staggering slightly from drinking too much, I lit the lamp, stripped to the waist, hurled myself onto the bed, closed one eye, then the other, and tried to fall asleep. But all was in vain. I felt drowsy, stiff, cataleptic, powerless to move; the blankets weighed on my back, enveloped me, fettered me as if they were cast iron; and during that drowsiness, I began to become aware that some singular phenomena were occurring around me.

The wick of the candle, which seemed to have gone out although made of pure stearine, was spewing coils of smoke so dense and black that gathering at the ceiling, they hid it and assumed the appearance of a cloak heavy as lead. The atmosphere of the room, having suddenly become stifling, was infused with an odor similar to the exhalations of burning flesh, my ears were deafened by an incessant rumbling the causes of which I could not divine, and the kneecap, which I saw there among my papers, seemed to move and spin on the surface of the desk, as if subject· to strange, violent convulsions.

I do not know how long I remained in that attitude: I could not remove my attention from the kneecap. My senses, faculties, ideas were all concentrated on that object; everything drew me to it. I wanted to sit up, get out of bed, leave, but it was not possible; and my distress reached such a pitch that I was almost not afraid—until the smoke emanating from the candle suddenly dissipated, I saw the curtain over the door rise, and the ghost I was expecting appeared.

I did not bat an eye. Having advanced to the center of the room, it bowed courteously and said to me, "I am Pietro Mariani, and I have come to take back my kneecap, as I have promised you."

And since my terror made me hesitant to answer him, he continued to speak in the most polite tones: "Pardon me if I must disturb you in the dead of night . . . at this hour . . . I realize that this is not a convenient time . . . but—"

"Oh, it is nothing, nothing at all!" I interrupted, reassured by so much courtesy. "In fact, I ought to thank you for your visit . . . I shall forever hold myself honored for having welcomed you into my home . . ."

"I am grateful for your cordiality," said the ghost, "but I wish, in any case, to explain the insistence with which I have demanded my kneecap, both from you and from the distinguished doctor from whom you received it. Observe."

And so saying, he lifted the edge of the white sheet in which he was wrapped and showed me that because he was missing the kneecap of his left leg, the shinbone was tied to the femur by a black ribbon passed two or three times through the opening of the fibula. Then he took several paces about the room in order to demonstrate how the absence of that bone prevented him from walking freely.

"Heaven forbid," I said in a mortified tone, "that the worthy former employee of the University of Pavia should be lame on my account! Your kneecap is over there, on the desk; take it, and mend your leg as best you can."

The ghost bowed for the second time in a gesture of gratitude, untied the ribbon that joined the femur to the shin, placed that make-shift remedy on the desk, and having picked up the knee-cap, began to adjust it to the leg.

"What news do you bear from the other world?" I then asked, seeing that the conversation was languishing during his task.

Instead of answering my question, however, he exclaimed with a saddened expression on his face, "This kneecap is rather deteriorated; you have not taken good care of it."

"I do not believe I have," I said, "but can it be that your other bones are more sound?"

He fell silent again and bowed a third time to bid me farewell. When he reached the doorway, however, he answered me as he closed the door behind himself, "Feel whether my other bones are not more sound."

After uttering these words, he stamped the floor so violently that all the walls shook, and at that noise I started and . . . woke up.

As soon as I was awake, I realized that it was the porter who was knocking on the door, saying, "It's me, get up, come and let me in."

"My God!" I exclaimed, rubbing my eyes with the back of my hands. "It was a dream, then, nothing more than a dream! How frightened I was! Thank heaven . . . But what nonsense! To believe in spiritualism . . . in ghosts . . ." Having hurriedly slipped into my trousers, I ran to open the door; and since the cold was counseling me to rush back to the blankets, I approached the desk to put the letter the porter had brought under the paperweight.

Yet how terrified I was when I saw that the kneecap had disappeared, and in its place I found the black ribbon Pietro Mariani had left there!

[1869]

The Lake of the Three Lampreys
(A Popular Tradition)

L A SILA IS a colossal forest in Southern Italy. Its holm oaks, ancient as the world, its swarthy, centuries-old larches, its common oaks, venerable with majesty, invest it with a frightening, savage appearance. These trees grow alone here, uncultivated, untouched by human hand. Here nature is sad and solitary, and a dreadful silence prevails. Only in the final hours of the day, near sunset, does the eagle sometimes rise amidst the trees and clouds to turn his solemn, measured circles and emit his melancholy shriek from on high, while packs of youthful wild boar crash through the thickets, splitting the saplings and rousing all the echoes of the forest. Here is no bird's flight, no woodsman's song. If you sound your voice, a long, sustained echo repeats your words. It seems as if this sound reverberating in the vault of the towering oaks will never fade, evoking an emotion akin to fear in any person who occasions it. These places are memorable for their antiquity and their popular traditions. Here flows the old Busento, whose waters bathe Cosenza and have roared over Alaric's grave in the nearby Crati Valley for fourteen hundred years. (He had such a magnificent tomb in this riverbed: they diverted the current and excavated an elegant sitting room, closer to a bridal suite than a grave, and after lowering the king into it, they brought back the waters.) From there extends the forest with its huge linden and white plane trees. At first, the trees grow sparsely and without underbrush like garden trees, and the surrounding area is inhabited by small birds, charming robins with their mobile tails, hopping yellow wagtails, and wrens the size of butterflies. Near these trees, several streams, with sources that lie somewhere in La Sila's still unexplored cliffs, create foaming waterfalls and small pools, whose banks are populated by frogs, thin green snakes, large speckled lizards, and little ribbon-shaped tarantulas, all content to dwell in those delicious, solitary margins. Within the wood, however, the spectacle is different, harsher, and more imposing. A light rustling of leaves now and then is the sign of a wild goat passing by, unobserved; an indistinct sound of voices is the confident, malicious yelping of wolves, and a harmony suffused with harplike melancholy is the buzzing of a bee or a dancing dragonfly. Here nature seems to have gathered what is most charming and most terrifying.

On one occasion, I entered this forest, and without realizing that I was traveling a very long distance, I found that I had penetrated deeply among the trees, and the sun was about to set. I became aware of the time from the last rays of sunlight, which obliquely colored the broad leaves of the alder and oak trees. Reluctantly, I prepared to return, anxious about the night and my unfamiliarity with the place. I had, moreover, already taken many steps toward the clearing. The path appeared to me and certainly was the same. I flattered myself with the thought that I had nearly reached the neighboring cotton fields, when having stopped to pick a certain flower that caught my eye, I noticed that I was still in the very place I had just left! Worried—no, astonished at this development—I retraced the same path for the second time; the thought of being overtaken by nightfall in that forest was frightening me—I walked with precipitate steps, it looked as if the trees were thinning out, I had a private laugh at my dismay and stopped to see how much distance remained to be traversed. But . . . oh, no! Who would believe it? I still had not moved a single step. I found myself precisely in the original place where I had resolved to turn back.

"This is without doubt an incomprehensible fate," I said to myself. "I shall not be able to return until tomorrow, I shall spend an entire night here, and heaven knows what will happen!"

Thus, I sat down along the path, entrusting myself to my destiny, and without in the least despairing that someone returning from the forest would rescue me from my solitude. I did not have to wait long. In fact, I soon discerned a woman coming toward me, traveling down my own path. Here a romantic storyteller would not hesitate to introduce us to a comely farm girl, a wood nymph, or who knows what. Yet she was no more than an ordinary woman, a country woman, with a sweet smile and vivacious southern eyes.

"Good Cosenzian," I said to her, "would you show me the path that leads out of this forest? I have been here for many hours, and I cannot figure out how to get back."

Instead of answering me at once, she lowered her eyes to the ground and turned about as if she wanted to find something she had mislaid. Then, with a peculiar smile, so incomprehensible as to reduce science to Johann Kaspar Lavater's mystical physiognomics, she said to me, "Are you a foreigner?"

"I am," I replied. "Why do you ask?"

"You have stepped on the malign herb. It grows in great quantities near these circles and around the lake of the three lampreys. Follow me, if you like, and I will lead you out of the forest."

This reply piqued in me all the curiosity of an inexperienced traveler.

"Here is a pleasant development," I said to myself. "What do you mean by malign herb? And what are these circles, this lake? I do not see any of these things."

"Observe," she resumed, and bending to the ground, she plucked several leaves from the foot of a tree. "Here is a stem. This is the malign herb. It grows for the most part around these circles, which we call witches' circles. Do you see these swarms of flies dancing over it with weary wings? And these lizards wandering around it constantly? Their destiny is decided, they will die here, because they will be unable to draw away from it. You yourself would have remained here a long time if I had not met you, and you might have died if this had happened in an unfrequented place. When someone steps on the malign herb and he has never heard of this herb, he is no longer able to leave the place where he happens to be, and it is necessary for another person, who first makes the sign of the cross three times (the same as the number of lampreys in the lake), to lead him back to the place where he set out. That person, however, will not be able to save more than seven others from this danger during her entire life. You are my first one, and I am most happy to render you this service."

I examined the herb carefully. It had the same leaves and the same shade of green as the yellow buttercup (*Ranunculus sceleratus*, Linnaeus), and the alleged witches' circles were only circular elevations in the earth with much greener and thicker grass, the same circles recalled by many travelers and named "greensour ringlets" by the English. They occur frequently in many parts of Europe, particularly on British beaches.

"The shepherds," the woman continued, "are most careful not to let the goats go near the herb, since they would not give milk anymore. Only merino sheep can graze there without harm. Do you also wish to visit the lake of the lampreys? Many people come to see it every day. It is not very far from our path, and on our way back to the town, I shall tell you the story of this lake. It is a most singular story."

In a few minutes we arrived at that pool, since it is not reasonable to call it a lake. Truly, its appearance was rather sad, despite the clearness of its waters. The only ornaments on its banks were some fuchsia scattered here and there, nightshade and rushes, and some common water lilies.

"This is the miraculous lake," the woman resumed. "Draw closer to the bank and look carefully now: do you not see the three lampreys?"

"I cannot see anything."

"That is not strange, because they tend to multiply or vanish when they are observed. This was the punishment meted out to guilty men. Let us get closer to the town, night is not far off, and I shall tell you the story of these lampreys.

"My mother, who came from the village of Nogliana, told me that about four hundred years ago this forest had already existed from time immemorial, yet to enter it was difficult and dangerous. The wild boars killed children, the eagles snatched the merinos and the geese, the circles and the malign herb grew in such great quantities that they detained travelers who were never seen returning. At that time, the villagers needed to erect a church, and there were several people who recommended that it be built within La Sila; thus, they hoped to avoid the impediments of nature with a sacred place, and this counsel was accepted. A church and a monastery were erected where a small spring previously stood. In this way, the forest was free and consecrated, and the poor people easily gathered sorb apples and wild grapes, much to the improvement of their condition. But the three hermits who went to live in the monastery were perverted men, and their impious and extraordinary deeds were recounted. Not much time had passed when a long drought dried the waters of the wells and springs. The sands in the river were burning, brooks were parched, trees withered, men and birds died. In this frightful state of things, only the spring at the church in the forest had not dried up; it still gave some trickles of water, and dying men gathered here from afar, seeking one more hour of life. Nevertheless, it did not take many days before this spring too gave only a few drops, and the three hermits who were living in the monastery walled up their doors in order to reserve this treasure for themselves alone. In vain did the thirsty come to beg a single, paltry sip of water; they died unsuccored near the walls of the sanctuary. But listen how the Lord's punishment could strike down the guilty. One evening an old pilgrim appeared among the others; he had a venerable countenance, and a long, snow-white beard descended down to his waist. He knocked at the monastery door and implored a hermit, who had looked out of the window, for a single drop of water, since he was on the verge of dying. The hermit was adamant in his refusal and closed the window in a fury. On the next morning, however, while everyone despaired of living any longer, the wells and springs began to gush so much water that the streets were flooded, the rivers exceeded their banks, and the forest brooks covered the meadows like lakes. Then the curate of Cirò immediately ordered a procession; everyone went to the monastery to celebrate such a great miracle, and . . . would you believe it? They looked for the church but the church was no longer there; the monastery had also disappeared; and where that spring existed they found the lake with the three lampreys, which you have seen. Those lampreys were the three hermits in the monastery, and that pilgrim was the Lord."

[1868]

The Elixir of Immortality
(In Imitation of the English)

16 DECEMBER 1867.—This is a most memorable anniversary for me. Today I complete my three hundred and twenty-ninth year of life.

Am I perhaps the wandering Jew?

No. More than eighteen centuries have accumulated on his head; in comparison to him, I am still quite young.

Quite young! But shall I never grow old, then? Am I truly immortal? This is a question that I have pondered indefatigably for three hundred and twenty-nine years now, and I still cannot answer it. This very day I discovered a gray hair on my head, a discovery which might induce me to believe that I am beginning to age . . . Yet it may have in fact remained hidden there for three hundred years; after all, many people are positively white before twenty.

I would like to relate my story.

By writing these pages I shall contrive to waste several hours of this my long existence, this eternity that has grown so wearisome to me. Eternity! Forever! Can it be? To live forever! I have often heard of enchantments endowed with the power of producing a profound sleep, a drowsiness lasting many centuries, after which the people who were its victims awoke as youthful as before. I have also heard discourses on the Seven Sleepers: this species of immortality could not be so oppressive; the certainty of an end had to lighten the burden of such a prolonged existence. But . . . alas! To live forever, forever! To live a life that cannot end! To witness this tedious passage of the hours in their slow, silent, serene succession! Ah! It is all too terrible!

But let us proceed to my narrative.

There is no one, I believe, who has not heard of Cornelius Agrippa. His memory is as immortal as his artifices have rendered yours truly immortal. The fame of his prodigies has spanned the centuries, just like his prodigies themselves—I who have lived for three hundred and twenty-nine years bear witness to this fact.

Many people have also heard of his pupil who, having inadvertently conjured up a malign spirit in his master's absence, was killed by it before anyone could come to his aid. The report of this accident, whether true or false, was accompanied by many inconveniences for the renowned philosopher. All his scholars abandoned him at once; his servants disappeared. He did not have a single man near him to heap coal on his always blazing fires while he slept or to observe the changing colors of his medicines while he stayed awake studying. All of his experiments failed, one after the other, because two hands were insufficient to complete them—the Prince of Darkness mocked him with the sneer that he was not capable of retaining a single mortal in his service.

I was then very young, very poor, and deeply in love.

I had been, for about a year, Cornelius's pupil, but I was absent when that disaster occurred. On my return, my friends entreated me not to return to the alchemist's house.

I trembled as I listened to the terrible tale they told me. I did not wait for a second warning: when Cornelius appeared to inquire about my work, offering me a full purse of gold if I consented to remain under his roof, I felt as if Satan himself had come to tempt me. I refused energetically and quickly evaded the philosopher's insistence by fleeing. Even on that occasion, my steps headed toward the place where they headed every night for two years—a place full of enchantments, a vast expanse of grassland with a spring whose water gushed forth in a melancholy gurgling. Next to this fountain sat a forlorn young girl, her radiant eyes fixed on the path I was accustomed to travel each day.

I cannot recall a moment in my life when I did not love Ortensia. We were childhood playmates; our affection was nurtured by habit. Her parents, like mine, were of very humble means, and for them our attachment had been the source of many pleasures, the occasion of many plans for the future. But misfortune did not delay in striking poor Ortensia, whose family was destroyed in a few months by a terrible epidemic—the girl was left an orphan.

She could have found help under my father's roof, but unfortunately the old gentlewoman of a nearby castle who had known her from infancy and was very wealthy, alone, and childless declared her intention to adopt her. Ortensia's happiness stopped us from opposing the lady's plans. From that day on, Ortensia lived in a sumptuous palace, dressed in luxurious clothing, commanded servants and carriages, and was considered a girl highly favored by fortune.

Nonetheless, in her new situation, among her new friends, she remained faithful to her humble childhood companion and frequently came to visit my father's cottage. And when forbidden to go there, she deliberately strayed into the forest and waited for me, seated at the edge of the fountain.

Quite often she declared to me that she did not feel bound to her new protectress by any duty equal in sanctity to that which bound us. Her attachment had surely not weakened, but I was too poor to take a wife, and she was weary of being tormented by my uncertainties.

Ortensia had a kind but haughty disposition, impatient with delays. The obstacles that opposed our union had also slightly cooled our hearts and proved to be the reason we did not see each other for quite some time.

I embraced her again after this very painful separation; the need for intimacy and solace had brought me back to her. She had not suffered any less during my absence; she complained bitterly about it to me and started to blame me, in effect, for being poor.

I responded rashly, "I am, however, honest, if I am poor; were I not, I would soon be rich!"

These imprudent words and the insistence with which she demanded an explanation of my meaning forced me to reveal the whole truth. Then, casting a disdainful look on me, she said, "You pretend to love me, but you fear to face these dangers for my love!"

I protested that in refusing Cornelius's offer I was counseled only by the dread of offending her. Although I knew I was lying, I insisted and swore that I would accept. Encouraged by her, provoked by shame, enticed by love and hope, nearly smiling at my previous fears, I returned to the alchemist with bold steps and a tranquil heart and was instantly installed in my office.

A year passed. I became the possessor of a considerable sum of money. Custom had banished my fears. In spite of the most painful vigilance, I had never detected the trace of a cloven foot, nor at any time was the melancholy silence of my sojourn disturbed by infernal screams. I still continued my prohibited interviews with Ortensia, and hope sat near me, deluding me—hope, but not perfect joy, since she fancied that love and absolute confidence in love were enemies, and she took pleasure in keeping them divided in my breast.

Although her heart was faithful, her behavior often possessed something light, something fatuous; her affability was so easy, so ready with everyone, that it made me jealous and was the ground of many terrible sufferings. She delighted in punishing me for it by accusing me of offenses I did not commit; and abusing the influence she exercised over me, she forced me to ask her forgiveness. She often fantasized that I was not sufficiently submissive, and then she would promptly trot out some stories of rivals favored by her protectress. Ortensia was surrounded by young men who were rich, happy, carefree, charming. With what kind of triumph could Cornelius's poor student flatter himself in competition with them?

On one occasion, the philosopher requested me to prolong my occupations near him, so that it was impossible for me to keep the rendezvous that was my daily custom.

He, meanwhile, was absorbed in a portentous undertaking which he had been working to complete for many years; and I was forced to remain at his side day and night, feeding the fires of his furnaces, watching over his chemical preparations. In vain did Ortensia await me at the fountain, and her proud spirit resented this neglect.

When I left the alchemist's workshop for an instant, during the few, very brief moments allotted to me for sleep, and dashed to our meeting place, hoping to be consoled by her, she welcomed me, then dismissed me with scorn. She vowed that her hand would be won by any other man but me—who could not be in two places at the same time for her love.

Ortensia wanted to be avenged—and truly she was. The news that she went on a hunting party escorted by Albert Koffer reached me in my workroom. Albert Koffer was favored by her protectress, and that very evening he, the gentlewoman, and Ortensia walked beneath the windows of my smoke-blackened dwelling. It seemed as if they were murmuring my name, as if Ortensia glanced inside my workroom with a scornful, derisive smile. At that instant, jealousy entered my breast with all its bitter poison, all its immense misery. At times, I shed torrents of tears, languishing at the thought that I could never call her mine; at others, I damned her inconstancy with a thousand curses.

And all the while I still had to stoke the alchemist's fires, still stay awake to observe the transformations of his incomprehensible philters.

Cornelius had watched for three days and nights. The progress of his alembics was slower than he flattered himself; despite his anxiety, sleep began to weigh heavily on his brows. Although countless times he fought against this fatal drowsiness with something stronger than a properly human effort, it still succeeded in lulling his senses into the most distressing impotence.

Cornelius looked at his clock. "It is still not ready," he said. "Will another night pass, then, before this work is perfected? Vincenzo, you are diligent, you are trustworthy, you have slept, my boy, you slept last night. Devote your attention to this glass vessel. The liquid it contains is a faint rose color; the instant this color begins to change, awaken me—until then, I can sleep. At first, it will turn white, and then emit some golden flashes. But do not wait until that moment; rouse me as soon as the rose color starts to fade." I barely heard these last words, murmured as they were, in sleep. Yet he did not yield completely to nature. "Vincenzo, my boy," he added, "do not touch the vessel, do not draw it to your lips; it is a philter—a philter to cure love; you will not want to cease loving your Ortensia—beware of drinking it."

Now he fell asleep. His venerable head sunk on his chest—I scarcely heard his regular, calm breathing. For several minutes I looked at the vessel: the liquid was still the same rose color. Then my attention was distracted by numerous thoughts that began to crowd my brain: I recalled the fountain where we usually met, the first days of our love, our childhood, my father's cottage, and I mused upon all those delightful scenes that would nevermore be renewed. Nevermore! My heart was rent by this word:

nevermore! Deceitful girl, false and cruel! She had never smiled at me as sweetly as she smiled at Albert that evening. Detested, vile creature! But I would not remain unavenged. Albert would breathe his last at her feet. Was it perhaps because she knew my weakness, because she sensed all the power she exercised over me, that she had smiled with that triumphant air as she passed beneath my windows? Yes, she realized her power, she knew that it could also provoke my hatred, my contempt, but not my indifference. Indifference! If only I could achieve so much, if only I could gaze on her with impassive eyes, and bestow my scorned love on someone else. Oh, that would be such a sweet victory!

At that moment, a bright beam flashed before my eyes. I had forgotten the alchemist's medicine. I observed it with amazement: flashes of marvelous beauty, more brilliant than those produced when diamonds are struck by the sun, glistened on the surface of the liquid. The most fragrant and gratifying scent I have ever smelled intoxicated all my senses. The vessel looked like a sphere of vibrant, eternal rays; the liquid it contained enticed me to lift it to my lips. Then I vividly recalled Cornelius's words: "It is a cure for love," he had told me. "You will not want to cease loving your Ortensia." "That would cure me of my passion," I exclaimed, "these dreadful pangs of love . . ." I seized the glass and, resolute, brought it to my lips. I had already drunk off half of the most delicious liquor ever tasted by the human palate when the philosopher suddenly awoke. I was startled, the vessel slipped from my hands, the liquor spread across the floor, emitting flashes of light and flame, while Cornelius shouted in a terrible voice, "Wretch! you have destroyed my entire life's work!"

The philosopher, however, was totally unaware that I had drunk any portion of his drug. He believed—and I did not want to disabuse him of this illusion—that I had lifted the vessel solely from curiosity, and hence frightened by his waking and by those flashes of extremely bright light, I had let it fall. I did not reveal the truth to him. The fire in the medicine was quenched, the fragrance faded, Cornelius grew calm again as a philosopher must when he has been tested by fortune, and he dismissed me with permission to take several days' rest.

I shall not attempt to describe the dream of glory and bliss that transported my spirit to heaven during the remaining hours of that memorable night. Words would be a futile, impotent expression of the joy that flooded my breast when I awoke from that slumber. I felt exalted; my thoughts were in heaven. Earth seemed heaven to me; a succession of infinite delights seemed to await me in the future.

"Thus it is to be cured of love," I thought. "Indifference is so sweet! Today I shall see Ortensia, today I shall be avenged on her scorn!"

The hours fled swiftly. The philosopher, confident that he would be successful on another occasion and trustful that he would have sufficient time to do it, began to concoct the same drug once again. He shut himself up with his books and his ingredients, and I had a few more days' vacation. I dressed with extreme care; I studied myself in the mirror, and it seemed to me that my eyes, once so ingenuous, had acquired a remarkable expression.

I hurried beyond the walls of the city with joy in my heart, with the proud satisfaction that accompanied the thought of being soon avenged. I headed toward the castle. I could now gaze on it without trembling, could observe its majestic towers with a calm, serene heart, because I felt cured of my love. Ortensia perceived me from afar as I wandered down an avenue. I know not what impulse suddenly animated her breast, but no sooner did she see me than she hurled herself down the stairs and ran headlong toward me. Yet she had been observed by someone else. Her protectress, that old, arrogant witch, the cause of all our misfortunes, had also come out of the castle and was running behind her, gasping and limping, waving her fan convulsively, with an equally horrid page carrying the train of her gown.

As if paralyzed by the lady's look, Ortensia clasped her hands and came to a halt, fixing her eyes upon me. She apparently wanted to implore my assistance and affection. I imagined the battle that was being waged in her soul. I hastened toward her.

What loathing I felt then for her protectress, that despicable old woman who wanted to smother the tender impulses of Ortensia's loving heart!

Until that moment, respect for the lady's rank had made me avoid her—I now disdained such trivial considerations. I was cured of love and lifted above every human fear. I approached Ortensia. How much affection shone in her face! Her eyes were flashing, her cheeks blazed with impatience and rage; she was a thousand times more charming, lovely, attractive. To see her was to feel myself rekindled. The change that then occurred in my heart was as instantaneous as the faith I had moments ago put in my supposed indifference.

That morning Ortensia had endured more tormenting vexations than usual, so that she would agree to give her hand immediately to my rival. She was accused of encouraging him with her demeanor and was threatened, if she refused, with expulsion from the castle. Her proud spirit was reawakened by that threat; and when she saw me, and recalled the injustice of her behavior toward me, and realized that she might have lost in me the only person she could consider a true friend, regret and indignation wrung tears from her. At that moment, I arrived.

"Oh! Vincenzo," she exclaimed, "lead me to your mother's cot, so that I can quickly abandon this abhorrent luxury, this gilded prison . . . Restore me to my poverty and happiness!"

Enraptured, I clasped her in my arms. The old woman could not utter a word, prevented as she was by agitation. A species of rage took possession of her; she burst into invective only when we were far on the road to my family's cottage. With transports of tenderness and joy, my mother welcomed the beautiful fugitive who had fled a gilded cage to resume her life in liberty and nature; my father, who loved her, gave her a hearty greeting. It was an hour of gladness, which did not require the addition of the alchemist's celestial potion to immerse me in pleasure.

Soon after that fortunate day, I became Ortensia's husband. I ceased to be Cornelius's pupil, but continued to be his friend. I always felt grateful to him for having unwittingly procured me that delicious draught of divine elixir, which, instead of curing me of love (insane cure! sad, desolate remedy for evils that are frequently recalled as blessings), armed me with courage and resolution to win a priceless treasure in my Ortensia.

With amazement I often recalled that period of ecstatic intoxication. Although Cornelius's drink did not achieve the purpose for which he asserted it had been prepared, its effects were more potent and delightful than words could express. These effects gradually diminished, but they still seemed to linger long, painting my life in the most gorgeous hues. Ortensia often marveled at my peace of mind and unusual cheerfulness, because my temperament had previously been rather serious and irascible. Her love grew with the transformation in my nature, and our days were winged with joy.

Five years later, I was suddenly summoned to the bedside of the dying Cornelius. He had me speedily fetched, entreating me to come to him without delay. I found him stretched out on his bed, afflicted by a deadly fever; all that remained of his life seemed to have fled to his piercing eyes, which were fixed on a small glass vessel filled with a roseate liquor.

"Behold," he said in a voice broken by gasps, "the vanity of human wishes! A second time my hopes were about to be crowned, and a second time they were destroyed. Look at that liquor. You recall that five years ago I prepared a similar potion, with the same result; then, as now, my greedy lips were impatient to drink the elixir of immortality! You put it beyond my reach! And now it is too late."

He spoke with difficulty and fell back on his pillow. I could not restrain myself from asking, "How, reverend master, could the cure for love ever restore you to life?"

He smiled sadly and said in scarcely intelligible words, "The cure you sought for your love destroyed the elixir of immortality. Ah! If now I might drink . . . I should live forever!"

As he spoke, a golden light flashed from the liquor, and a fragrance I well remembered suffused the air. Weakened as he was, he sat up; strength seemed to reanimate his body miraculously;

he extended a hand—a deafening explosion made me start—a blaze of fire suddenly leapt from the elixir, and the glass vessel that contained it shattered into a thousand atoms. I turned around—Cornelius had fallen back on his pillow—his eyes were glassy—his features rigid—he was dead.

Yet I survived him, and I lived, destined to live forever. So said the unfortunate alchemist, and for a few days I believed his words.

I remembered the glorious drunkenness that had followed the libation stolen from the philosopher's lips; I began to ponder the alterations I had subsequently observed in my body, in my soul: the marvelous elasticity of the one, the animated serenity of the other. I examined myself in a mirror and was unable to detect the slightest change in my features after the five years that had elapsed. I remembered the radiant hues and gratifying scent of that delicious beverage—the gift should equal the excellence of the giver—I was, therefore, immortal!

Several days later I smiled at my credulity. The hackneyed proverb that "a prophet is least regarded in his own country" was true as far as my master and I were concerned. I loved him as a man—I respected him as a sage—but I derided the view that he could command the powers of darkness, and I smiled at the superstitious errors with which he was regarded by the vulgar. He was a wise philosopher, but he had no relations with any spirit, except those clothed in flesh and blood. His science did not elevate him beyond human science; and I soon persuaded myself that any science deriving from man could not master the laws of nature so fully as to imprison a soul forever in its mortal coil.

Cornelius had concocted a soul-restoring drink; more inebriating than wine, sweeter and more fragrant than any fruit, it probably possessed strong medicinal qualities that imparted happiness to the heart and vigor to the limbs. But its effects had to fade with time; already they were diminished in my body. I was a lucky young fellow . . . I had imbibed health and joyous spirits, and perhaps a long life, at my master's expense; but my good fortune must have ended there: longevity is quite different from immortality.

I continued to entertain this illusion for several years. Occasionally, I was seized by a doubt—was the alchemist really deceived? But my habitual credence was that I too would meet the fate of all Adam's children at my appointed hour—a little late perhaps, but still at a natural age. It is undeniable, however, that I preserved a marvelously youthful appearance. I smiled at my vanity in consulting the mirror so often, but I consulted it to no effect: my brow was still free of wrinkles, my cheeks, my eyes, my entire person continued to remain as intact as in my twentieth year.

I was troubled. I saw Ortensia's beauty fade—I looked more like her son. By degrees, our neighbors began to make the same observations, and finally I noticed that because I had been Cornelius's student, I was thought to be a sorcerer. Ortensia herself entertained the same idea. She became jealous and peevish and at last turned quarrelsome. We had no children; we were everything to each other; and although, as she grew older, her vivacious spirit was a little mixed with her ill temper and her pitifully decayed beauty, I held her dear to my heart as the mistress I had once idolized, as the wife I had sought and won with my passionate love.

Finally, our situation turned intolerable: Ortensia was fifty years old—I was twenty. Shamefully I adopted in some measure the habits of a more advanced age. No longer did I mingle at dances with the young and happy: my heart leapt with them, but I halted my feet, and I assumed a pensive attitude among the Nestors of our village. Before the time I mention, however, things had changed—we were universally shunned—I was accused of having maintained guilty relations with several of my old master's alleged friends. Poor Ortensia was pitied, but abandoned. I was regarded with horror and detested.

What was to be done? We huddled near our fireplace, resigned to the solitude in which we now found ourselves, and prepared for the poverty that threatened us—for at this point no one would purchase the produce from my farm, and I was often forced to travel twenty miles to find some place where I was not known in order to sell my provisions. We had put something aside for a rainy day—that day has come.

We sat near our solitary fireplace—the old-hearted youth and his ancient wife. Again Ortensia insisted on knowing the truth; she recapitulated all the gossip she had ever heard whispered about me and added her own observations. She conjured me to reject sorcery; she described gray hair as much more refined than my chestnut locks; enraptured, she spoke of the reverence and respect due to advanced age—how much more preferable to the frivolous attention paid on mere childhood! Could I imagine that the vulgar graces of youth would be the cause of so many misfortunes? What more must be said? She predicted that I would be imprisoned, burned as a witch, while she, to whom I disdained to grant any portion of my good fortune, would be stoned as my accomplice. At length, she gave me to understand that I must share my secret with her and bestow on her the very benefits I myself enjoyed, or she would denounce me—and then she burst into tears.

In this distressing predicament, I thought that divulging the truth would be the best decision. And I revealed it as gently as possible and spoke only of a "very long life," not of immortality—belief that, in truth, accorded better with my ideas. When I finished, I rose and said, "And now, my Ortensia, will you denounce the lover of your youth? You will not, I know. But it is too hard a fate that you must be unhappy because of my wretched fortune and Cornelius's accursed arts. I shall leave you—you are wealthy enough, and the people who shunned you will renew their friendships in my absence. I shall go; young as I seem and vigorous as I am, I can work and earn my bread among strangers, where I shall arrive unsuspected and unknown. I loved you in youth; God is my witness that I would not want to desert you in old age did not your safety and happiness require it."

I took my hat and started toward the door; in an instant Ortensia's arms were encircling my neck, her lips pressing against mine. "No, my Vincenzo, my friend," she said, "you shall not go alone—take me with you; together we will abandon this village and, as you say, take refuge among strangers, unknown and safe. I am not so very old as to make you ashamed of me; and I dare hope that your beauty will soon fade, and you will begin to look more elderly, which in fact is more dignified. No, you do not want to abandon me."

I clasped her to my breast. "I shall not leave you, no, my Ortensia, my dear wife; without your love I would not have enough heart to leave you." The next day we secretly prepared for our emigration. We were forced to make great pecuniary sacrifices; it could not be helped. We realized a sum sufficient, at least, to provide for our maintenance while Ortensia lived, and without bidding adieu to a living soul, we abandoned our native country to seek refuge in a remote part of western France.

It was a cruel thing to go off like that, leaving our native village and the friends of our youth, repairing to an unknown country to live among strange people, with different customs.

The singular secret of my fate rendered me indifferent to this exile, but for her I felt profound compassion, and it gladdened me to perceive that she found recompense for her misfortunes in a variety of childish, ridiculous circumstances. Without alluding to them all, she sought to diminish the obvious disparity in our years with a thousand feminine artifices—rouge, youthful dress—and she adopted the behavior of an adolescent. I could not complain. Did not I myself wear a mask? Should I complain because she wore hers with less fortunate results? Rather, I grieved profoundly when I recalled that this was my Ortensia, whom I had loved so madly, whose affection I had won with such transports—the dark-eyed, dark-haired girl, with the arch, bewitching smile and the fawnlike step—this affected, untidy, jealous old woman. I should have reverenced her gray hair, her withered cheeks; I loved her—it was my duty, I realized—but I could not do less than pity this type of human degeneration.

Her jealousy never slept. Her principal occupation was discovering that, despite external appearances, I myself was aging. I truly believe that the poor thing sincerely loved me from the depths of her heart, but no woman in the world ever had a more tormenting mode of showing tenderness. She was consumed with finding wrinkles in my face and something halting or decrepit in my step, while I displayed only that exuberant vigor which appears in a youth of twenty. At no time did I dare court another woman. On one occasion, fancying that a girl in the village had looked on me with favorable eyes, she conjured me to cover my head with a gray wig.

The constant theme of her conversation was this—that although I looked so young, I possessed something that would cause me to age suddenly, and she maintained that the worst symptom was precisely my healthy appearance. My youth was an illness, she said, and I would always have to be prepared, if not for a sudden and terrible death, then at least to awake some morning with a wrinkled face, stooped shoulders, and all the signs of advanced years. I expressly let her natter away, and her conjectures often delighted me. Her warnings hung over my incessant meditations concerning my condition, and I took a passionate, if painful, interest in listening closely to everything that her spirited subtlety and excited imagination suggested to her on this topic.

Why should I dwell on these minute circumstances? We lived in this way for several long years. Ortensia became paralytic and could no longer rise from her bed; I sat up with her and nursed her like a mother. She grew peevish and always harped upon one string: how long I would survive her.

The awareness that I had scrupulously performed my every duty to her was a precious source of consolation to me. She had been mine in youth and was also mine in age; and finally, when I flung some lumps of earth on her corpse, I wept in the realization that with her I had lost all that really kept me connected to life.

Ever since then, how many were my cares and misfortunes, how few and vain my joys! I pause here in my story. I will pursue it no further. A sailor without rudder or compass, tossed on a tempestuous sea, a traveler lost on a limitless heath, without landmark or sign to guide him—such was I, more lost, more hopeless than either of them. A nearing ship, a glimmer from a distant cottage could yet save them, but I had only one hope, always desired and always ungranted—perhaps never to be granted—the hope that I would die. Death! Severe and mysterious friend of man. Why have you refused your refuge to me alone among all mortals? Oh! If only the sweet silence of the grave, the summoned peace of the tomb, would stop this thought from burning my brain, this heart from beating with emotions varied only by different forms of pain!

Am I immortal? I return to my question. In the first place, is it not more likely that the alchemist's drink possessed the virtue of conferring longevity, rather than eternity? Such is my hope. And then it is worth recalling, on the one hand, that I drank only half of the potion he had prepared. Was not the whole necessary to complete the spell? To have drained half of the elixir of immortality is to be but half-immortal—my "forever" is thus truncated and nullified.

On the other hand, however, who can number the years in a half-eternity? I often do my utmost to imagine by what rule the infinite may be divided. Occasionally, I fancy that age is overtaking me. I have found a gray hair. Madman! Do I complain? Yes, the fear of age and death often sends a chill to my heart, and the more I live, the more I am terrified of death, even when I feel that I abhor life. Such an enigma is man—born to die—and yet struggling, as I do, against the immutable laws of his nature.

But this very anomaly of feeling tells me that I can die: the alchemist's drug will be unable to withstand the test of fire, the sword, or the fury of the waves. I have fixed my gaze on the blue depths of some placid lake or on the tumultuous rushing of some mighty river and exclaimed: peace inhabits only these waters. All the same, I have turned my steps elsewhere, to live yet another day. I have asked myself whether suicide could be a crime for someone to whom the gates of another world can be opened only by this means. I have taken every risk, except that of putting my life to the test, except that of becoming, like a soldier or a duelist, a cause of my own and my fellow mortals' destruction. But they are not my fellows. The inextinguishable power of life in my mechanism and their ephemeral existence place us as far apart from one another as the poles. I cannot lift a hand against the vilest or the most powerful among them.

Thus have I lived for many years—alone and bored with myself—longing for death and yet always living—a mortal immortal. Neither ambition nor avarice has ever invaded my spirit, and the passionate love that consumes my heart, never to be returned—I never discovered an equal affection to which I could devote myself—remains there only to torture me.

On this very day, I have devised a plan by which I shall put an end to everything, without making myself my own executioner, without making myself a Cain—it is an expedition that a mortal frame could not in any way survive, even if animated by the youth and strength that still reside in mine. In this way shall I put my immortality to the test: if this test prevails, I shall find peace forever; if it yields, I shall become an object of wonder and be considered one of the great benefactors of the human species.

Before I depart, a miserable vanity has induced me to pen these pages. I do not want to die without leaving a name behind me. Three centuries have past since I drank that fatal potion; another year will not elapse before, encountering gigantic dangers, struggling against the germs that death holds within itself, harried by privation, exhaustion, and battle, I shall abandon this body—prison too narrow for a soul that yearns for freedom—to the destructive elements of air and water. But if I am permitted to survive, my name will be recorded as one of the most famous among the sons of men; and having completed my mission, I shall adopt more resolute means. By scattering and annihilating the atoms that compose my mechanism, I shall set free the life that lies imprisoned within and is so cruelly hindered from soaring above this dismal earth to a world more congenial to its immortal essence!

[1865]

The Letter U
(A Madman's Manuscript)

U! U!
Have I written this terrible letter, this frightening vowel? Have I delineated it precisely? Have I traced it in all its awful exactitude—its fatal outline, its two detested shafts, its abhorrent curve? Have I carefully inscribed this letter, whose sound makes me shudder, whose sight fills me with terror?

Yes, I have written it.

And here it is again:

U

And again:

U

Look at it, stare unblinkingly at it—do not tremble, do not blanch—muster up the courage to bear the sight of it, to observe all its parts, to examine all its details, to conquer all the horror that inspires in you . . . This U! . . . This fatal sign, this odious letter, this dreadful vowel!

Have you seen it now? . . . But what am I saying? . . . Who among you has not seen it, written it, pronounced it millions of times?—I know this, but I shall ask you all the same. Who among you has examined it? Who has analyzed it? Who has studied its form, expression, influence? Who has made it the object of his inquiries, pursuits, vigils? Who has been absorbed by it every day of his life?

Because . . . in this sign you see only a meek letter, innocuous like the others; because habit has rendered you indifferent to it; because your apathy has deterred you from studying its features more accurately . . . Yet I . . . If only you knew what I have seen! . . . If only you knew what I see in this vowel!

U

Now consider it with me.

Look at it carefully, look at it attentively, dispassionately, stare! And so: what have you to say about it?

That line which curves and forks—the two shafts that look at you unmoving, that look at each other unmoving—the two dashes that cut them off inexorably, terribly—that lower arc, on which the letter rocks back and forth, sneering—and, on the inside, that blackness, that void, that horrible void staring from the opening of the shafts, rejoining and vanishing in the infinity of space . . .

But this is still nothing. Steel your nerves!

Redouble your powers of intuition; hurl yourself into your most penetrating gaze.

Set out from one of the two ends, follow the outer edge, descend, approach the arc, pass beneath it, ascend, reach the opposite end . . .

What did you see?

Wait!

Now make the journey in reverse. Descend the entire length of the line—descend with courage, vigorously—reach the base, halt, stop a moment, examine it attentively; then reascend to the point whence you set out in the beginning . . .

Do you not tremble? Grow pale?

It is still not sufficient!

Rest your eyes for a moment on the two dashes that cut off the shafts; look from one to the other; then look at the entire letter, look at it in one glance, examine it from every angle, grasp it in all its expressiveness . . . and tell me if you are not paralyzed, if you are not vanquished, if you are not annihilated by this sight?!?!

Look.

I write all the vowels here:

.   a e i o u

Do you see them? Do they look right at you?

Well, then?!

But it is not enough just to see them.

Now listen to their sounds.

A—The expression of sincerity, frankness, a slight but pleasant surprise.

E—kindness, tenderness expressed in a single sound.

I—What joy! What intense, profound joy!

O—What surprise! What wonder! And what a welcome surprise! What frankness in that letter, clumsy but manly!

Now listen to U. Pronounce it. Draw it from the depths of your thoracic cavity, but pronounce it carefully: *Yu! Yuh!! Yuhh!!! Yuhhh!!!!*

Do you not shudder? Do you not tremble at this sound? Do you not hear the roar of the wild beast, the moan uttered in pain, all the voices of suffering, shaken nature? Do you not sense something obscure, profound, infernal in that sound?

God! What a terrible letter! What a dreadful vowel!!

I want to tell you my life.

I want you to know how this letter drove me to crime and to an ignominious and unmerited punishment.

I was born doomed. A terrible sentence weighed on me from

the first day of my existence: my name contained a U. This fact is the source of every misfortune in my life.

At seven years old, I was sent to school.

An instinct, the causes of which I had not yet grasped, prevented me from learning that letter, from writing it. Every time they made me read the vowels, I stopped, unwillingly, in front of U; my voice failed me, an indescribable panic possessed me—I could not pronounce that vowel!

Writing it was worse! The hand that wrote the other letters so confidently convulsed and trembled whenever I set about to write this one. First the shafts converged too much, then diverged too much; sometimes they formed an upright V, sometimes they were overturned: Λ. I was unable to trace the curve in any way, and often I managed only to form a confused, meandering line.

The teacher gave me the ruler across the knuckles—I grew bitter and wept.

One day, when I was twelve years old, I saw a colossal U written on the blackboard, like this:

U

I was sitting in front of the blackboard. That vowel was there, and it seemed to be watching me, staring at me, challenging me. Somehow I was suddenly emboldened: I was certain that the moment of truth had arrived! That letter and I were enemies; I accepted the challenge, rested my chin on my hands, and began to look at it . . . Several hours passed as I sat there, poised in contemplation. It was then that I understood everything, saw everything I have now told you or at least tried to tell you, although to tell it exactly would be impossible. I divined the reasons for my repugnance and hatred; and I planned a fight to the death with that letter.

I began by taking as many of my schoolmates' books as I could and crossing out every U I saw. It was only the beginning of my vendetta. I was expelled from school.

Nonetheless, I returned later. My teacher's name was *Aurelio Tubuni*.

Three of them!! I abhorred him for this. One day I wrote on the blackboard: *Death to U!* He saw himself as the object of that threat. I was again expelled.

I was permitted to return a second time. I then proposed, as a research topic, a project relating to the abolition of this vowel, to its banishment from the letters of the alphabet.

I was not understood. I was branded a lunatic. My schoolmates, having thus become aware of my aversion to that vowel, began a terrible war against me. I saw, I found U everywhere: they wrote the letter all over my books, the walls, the benches, the blackboard—my notebooks, my papers were covered with it. Nor could I defend myself against this bitter, atrocious persecution.

One day in my pocket I found a card on which a long row of them was written in this infernal number:

U U U U U U U U

I was enraged! The sight of U arrayed in this guise, placed in this awful gradation, pushed me to the edge. I felt the blood rushing to my head, confusing my thinking . . . I ran to school, and having seized one of my schoolmates by the throat, I would have surely choked him to death if he had not been removed from my hands.

It was the first crime that vowel provoked from me!

I was stopped from continuing my studies.

Then I began to live by myself, to think, meditate, work by myself. I entered a new sphere of observations, a more elevated, more active sphere: I studied the relations that linked the destiny of humanity to this fatal letter. I found every thread, discovered every cause, intuited every law; and during five long years of labor, I wrote and produced a voluminous work wherein I proposed to demonstrate that every human calamity proceeded from no other cause than the existence of U and from the use we make of U in writing and speech, but also that it was possible to suppress it, to discover a remedy and prevent the evils that threaten us.

Would you believe it? I could not find the means to bring my work into the world. Society refused my offer of the only cure that could still save it.

When I was twenty years old, I burned with love for a young woman, and my love was reciprocated. She was divinely good, divinely beautiful. We fell in love at first sight, and when I could speak to her, I asked, "What is your name?"

"Ulrica!"

"*Ulrica!*—U." A U! It was horrible. How could I subject myself to the constant, dreadful violence of that vowel? My love was everything to me, but I nevertheless found the strength to renounce it. I abandoned Ulrica.

I tried to cure myself with another emotional involvement. I gave my heart to another girl. Would you believe it? I later learned that her name was *Giulia*. I parted company with her as well.

I had a third love. My experience had made me cautious: I inquired about her name before I gave her my heart.

Her name was *Annetta*. Finally! We prepared for the wedding; everything had been arranged, settled, when, as I was examining her birth certificate, I discovered, to my horror, that Annetta was no more than a pet name, a diminutive of *Susanna, Susanetta,* and what is even more horrible, she had five other Christian names: *Postumia*, *Uria*, *Umberta*, *Giuditta*, and *Lucia*.

Imagine how I felt myself shudder when reading those names! In an instant I tore apart the nuptial contract, confronted that perfidious monster with her ruthless betrayal, and left that house forever. Heaven had saved me once again.

But alas! I could no longer love, my sensibility was exhausted, debilitated by so many terrible experiences. Chance brought me back to Ulrica. The memories of my first love were reawakened, my passion was rekindled with new fervor . . . I still wanted to renounce her affection, and the happiness that this affection once again promised me . . . but I did not have the strength—we were married.

At that moment, my struggle commenced.

I could not tolerate her bearing a U in her name, could not call her by that word. My wife! . . . My companion, the woman I loved—with a U in her name?! . . . She who had already made such a terrible purchase in mine, since there was even one in my surname!

It was impossible!

One day I told her, "My beloved, you see how terrible this U is. Renounce it! Shorten or change your name! . . . I implore you."

She smiled and did not reply.

Once again I told her, "Ulrica, your name is unbearable to me . . . it makes me ill . . . it is killing me! Renounce it."

My wife smiled again, the ingrate! She smiled! . . .

One night I felt myself possessed by a strange frenzy: I had had an upsetting dream . . . A gigantic U was sitting on my chest and embracing me with its two immense, supple shafts . . . squeezing me . . . crushing and crushing me . . . I leapt from the bed, incensed. I seized my hefty sword cane, ran to a notary, and told him, "Come, come with me this instant, you must draft a formal writ of renunciation . . ."

The wretch resisted. I dragged him from me, dragged him to my wife's bed.

She was sleeping. I woke her roughly and said, "Ulrica, renounce your name, the detestable U in your name!"

My wife stared at me in silence.

"Renounce it," I repeated in a terrible voice. "Renounce that U . . . Renounce your abhorrent name!!"

She still stared at me and was silent!

Her silence, her refusal put me beside myself; I hurled myself on her and beat her with my stick.

I was arrested and brought to trial for this act of violence.

The judges, although their verdict was acquittal, sentenced me to a more terrible punishment—detention in a mental hospital.

I, mad! The bastards! Mad! Because I had discovered the secret of their destinies! Their adverse destinies! Because I had endeavored to improve them? . . . Ingrates!

Yes, I feel that this ingratitude will kill me—left alone here, defenseless! Face to face with my enemy, with this detested U that I see every hour, every moment, asleep, awake, in every object that surrounds me, I feel that I will finally have to succumb.

So be it.

I do not fear death; I hasten it as the only end to my woes.

I would have been happy if I could have benefited humanity, persuading men to suppress that vowel—or if it had never existed, or if I had not fathomed its mysteries.

It has been decided otherwise! Perhaps my misfortune will prove a useful lesson to men; perhaps my example will spur them to imitate me . . .

I can only hope so!

May my death precede by a few days the epoch of their great emancipation, their emancipation from U, from this terrible vowel!!!

The unhappy man who wrote these lines died in the insane asylum of Milan on 11 September 1865.

[1869]

The Fated

DO THERE REALLY exist beings destined to exercise a malign influence over men and the things that surround them? This is a truth that we witness every day, but our coolly practical reason, trained to accept only those facts that fall under the sway of our senses, is always loathe to admit it.

If we examine all our actions carefully, even the most ordinary and inconsequential, we shall nonetheless see that they do not include any which dissuades us from this belief, or whose performance has not in some manner provoked it. This superstition enters every event in our lives.

Many people believe that they can shield themselves from it by maintaining, precisely, that it is no more than superstition. Yet they do not perceive that they thus reduce it to a simple question of words. This reduction would not undermine the belief, since superstition also requires faith.

We cannot fail to recognize that in the spiritual world as in its physical counterpart, everything that happens, happens and changes through certain laws of influence whose secrets we remain unable to divine entirely. We observe the effects, and we continue to be stupefied and ignorant before the causes. We see the influence of things over things, of intelligences over intelligences, of the former over the latter, and vice versa; we see all these influences intersect, exchange, work on one another, reuniting in a single center of action these two very disparate worlds, the world of spirit and the world of matter.

We have borne our faith as far as human discernment has penetrated; the secret of physical phenomena is partly violated; science has analyzed nature; nearly every natural process, law, and influence is known to us. Yet science has come to a standstill before psychological phenomena and before the relationships that join them to nature. It has not been able to advance any further and has restrained our beliefs at the threshold of this unexplored kingdom. We can admit general theses and complex truths in the order of facts, but not in the order of ideas.

Where facts are uncertain, ideas are confused. Facts occur that do not present a fixed, perceptible, well-defined character, and that our calculating reason is doubtful whether to deny or admit. As a result, there are fragmentary, obscure, unstable ideas, which can never present themselves unequivocally, and which we are uncertain whether to accept or reject. This uncertainty of facts, this fragmentation of ideas, this vague state between a firm and a wavering faith perhaps constitute what we call superstition—the point of departure for all great truths, the first embryonic concept of all great beliefs.

If I see a superstition seize the spirit of the masses, I say that deep within it resides a truth, since we do not have ideas without facts, and this superstition can issue only from a fact. If the fact has not yet been replicated and generalized to confirm the superstition, the reason is that the path of humanity stretches far and wide—more so than that of things—and no one can determine the time and circumstances which would make possible such a replication. Men have adopted a facile, logical system as regards conventions—they admit what they see, deny what they do not see—but until now this system has not prevented them from later admitting quite a few truths they initially denied. Scientific progress bears witness to it. However that may be, there is no person whose belief in the influences that men and things can exercise over us has not been more or less strengthened, illuminated and confirmed by his own experience. At the most it is a question not of denying this belief—since its existence is indisputable—but of learning its raison d'être and the extent to which it must be accepted.

I find proof of it everywhere. For me, antipathy is only a tacit awareness of the fatal influence that one person can exercise over another. In the ignorant masses, this awareness has created the "evil eye"; in the educated masses, prejudice, mistrust, suspicion.

There is nothing more common than hearing exclamations like "I do not like that man; I would not want to meet him on the street; he frightens me; in his presence I turn into a nonentity; whenever I run into that man, some misfortune befalls me." Nor is this belief, which presents itself under so many guises, which we nearly fail to notice, which is virtually innate in us like all the defensive instincts nature has given us, held exclusively by a small group of people—it is, in greater or lesser proportions, everyone's natural inheritance.

This superstition accompanies humanity from childhood and is diffused through all peoples. Men of genius, those who have suffered much, have put greater faith in it than others. The number of persons who have believed that they were persecuted by a fatal being is infinite; it is equal to the number of persons who have believed that they themselves were fatal beings: Hoffmann, who was kind and loving, was tortured his entire life by this thought.

There is no point in dwelling on it, since history is full of such examples, and each of us can find evidence for this almost instinctive belief in our private lives.

I do not want to demonstrate its absurdity or its truth. I believe that no one can do either with authoritative arguments. I limit myself to recounting facts that pertain to this superstition.

During carnival in 1866 I found myself in Milan. It was Shrove Tuesday, and the procession of maskers had grown very animated. I must, however, draw a distinction—animated with spectators, not with maskers. The charge of unworthy renown, so frequent and so just in art, can also be applied to popular festivals, and the carnival of Milan would undoubtedly deserve it. These festivals are nothing more than a mystification, and they have every reason to be, since the thousands of foreigners who annually attend them are not any less convinced that they are having an enjoyable experience. Everyone instills in themselves the conviction that carnival in Milan is the most comical, witty, diverting thing in the world. Once this belief is introduced, facts are no longer necessary to confirm it—the goal of diversion is attained.

Carnival in 1866 was not any less animated than at other times, and in the first hours of nightfall on this last Tuesday before Lent, people poured into the streets in torrents. The crowd packed the thoroughfares so tightly that at several points movement was impossible, and near the intersection of Via San Paolo, where I was, we were literally crushed.

The honest Milanese mingled with the foreigners in a brotherly way and were intoxicated with the pleasure of looking into the whites of one another's eyes—which constitutes the sole but sublime diversion of this celebrated carnival.

151

I do not know how long I had been standing there, amid that great throng, in a most uncomfortable position, when turning about to see if there were some exit, I observed an extremely curious spectacle near me.

The crowd had not thinned out but condensed so as to create a rather large circular space in its midst. At the center of this miraculous circle stood a young man who seemed not more than eighteen years old, but who, when examined more carefully, could have been taken for twenty-five, so sickly did his face appear, so deeply etched with the traces of a long and troubled life. He was blond and very handsome, excessively thin, but not so much that the beauty of his features was diminished. He had large blue eyes, and his lower lip slightly protruded, although it was more expressive of sadness than rancor. His entire appearance possessed something feminine, delicate, ineffably graceful—a quality that the French call *souple*, and that I could not express any better with a different word from our language. The purity and harmony of his lines were amazing; he was dressed with extreme elegance; and he was looking about with a melancholy, distracted air, sometimes at the crowd, sometimes at the maskers, as if he were there against his will and more interested in himself than in the less attractive spectacle he found before his gaze.

But what struck me as most remarkable was that he seemed not to notice the circle that formed around him, nor did any of the people who formed it. There was nothing truly extraordinary about it; yet the existence of a space so vast in the midst of a crowd so dense, in the midst of a multitude that moved, trembled, undulated like a single body, without ever filling the void formed at that point, seemed to me worthy of attention. It could be said that the young man emitted a repulsive fluid, a mysterious power capable of distancing everything that surrounded him.

At the moment when I was looking at him, as he was being showered with some sugared almonds, quite a lot of them catching in the folds of the cloak he kept draped over his arm, a little boy broke away from the circle and approached him as if to ask about the sweets, since the young man had neither brushed them away nor shaken his cloak to make them fall.

He looked at the boy affectionately, gathered the almonds, gave them to him, and before the boy left, the man ran a hand through the boy's hair in a tender gesture imbued with gentleness and melancholy.

He put so much affection into that gesture that even if nature had not endowed him with such a sweet and sympathetic face, he would have been immediately judged kind and courteous.

The fact is that the face is the mirror of the soul. It is impossible to know whether nature herself gives a good expression to the good and an evil one to the evil, or whether human goodness and evil can so work on our countenance as to alter it and stamp it with their seal. It is most certain, however, that the heart shines through our features, even through those whose beauty seems to hide a base soul or whose ugliness an honest one.

I would have never tired of looking at him. I do not know whether the affections of other men are governed by the law of sympathies and antipathies—sudden, forceful, inexorable— to which mine are subject; for me, falling in love with a man or woman, entertaining an irresistible fondness or aversion for any creature has never taken more than a few minutes to happen. Thus, I recall that so tender was the expression on his face, so directly had that language spoken to my heart, that I would have embraced him there on the street without giving reason the opportunity to debate it.

I did not move from that spot until he too moved. The festival began to slacken, the crowd was dispersing, and twilight enfolded the entire scene in a heavy gray light. We were a few steps from a café, and he entered it with the air of a man who does not know how to spend his time, who feels the weight of his arms, his legs, his whole body, and would like to rid himself of it, throwing it on a divan like an annoying, useless bundle. I was in the same situation, I did not have a thing to do, and I followed him.

We sat facing one another, with me watching him reading. Yet he seemed so little interested in his reading that even if he had grasped the newspaper upside down, I believe he would not have noticed. His eyes were fixed on the columns of newsprint, but they seemed to look within rather than out, seemed to concentrate all their visual power in themselves, and were concerned only with what was happening in the young man's soul.

No sooner had I made this observation than I noticed another throng of people at the café window and heard what sounded like women screaming. I was about to rise as the door opened, and a boy was carried inside, unconscious: he had been run down by a carriage and suffered a broken leg. I was painfully shocked to recognize that this was the very boy whom the unknown man had caressed in the middle of that circle and to whom he had given the sweets that fell on his cloak.

I instinctively turned my gaze toward the man and glimpsed him in the instant that he hurried from the room. His face, reflected in a mirror hanging before me, seemed very pale.

I quit the café not much later, prey to sad thoughts.

On that very evening an extraordinary performance was to take place at La Scala.

The opera scheduled was *La Sonnambula*, and people flocked to hear that divine music, so rich, so complex in its simplicity, so tender. *L'Africaine* had been performed a little while ago—from Meyerbeer to Bellini, the difference, if not the distance, was very great. The theater was brightly lit, the orchestra densely packed with listeners, and there remained only five or six empty boxes, all situated in the same place. I noticed, much to my surprise, that one of them contained the young man I had just seen viewing the procession of the maskers.

He was alone and no longer looked sad or pensive to me. He wore a very elegant black suit, but without appearing as if he usually took great care with his appearance. I do not know whether it was my delusion, or hallucination, or something else, but he seemed to me extraordinarily handsome, much more so than a few hours earlier.

His face had a radiant quality, one resembling the intense transparency, however much cloudy or veiled, that characterizes alabaster. He did indeed have the same pallor; without looking into his eyes, without examining the wonderful liveliness of his features, one might have thought he was dead or petrified. His hair still retained that fineness, that pliancy and sheen, that simple, natural curl found in children's hair; it was a marvelous blond and shone like golden threads with the reflection of the flames from the candelabra. He was leaning his elbow on the railing, his cheek in his hand; with his head inclined in this fashion, he seemed even more beautiful. He had the sort of beauty women have: it derives a mysterious, fascinating authority from the light. To behold him from the orchestra—whence the rest of his body could not be seen—one would have thought the head, so diaphanous and white, belonged to a boy, a fragile, delicate creature, perhaps a supernatural being.

I alone remarked the strange relationship between this scene and my previous observation at the procession of the maskers—I mean my discovery of him so isolated, surrounded by five or six empty boxes, while it was impossible to find a single unoccupied box anywhere else in the theater; for one to feel amazement before this fact, it is necessary to have first observed the phenomenon of the circle. The audience was unanimous, however, in noticing and admiring his beauty, and it did not take me long to realize that the ladies were especially struck by it and vied in aiming their opera glasses in his direction.

Among the girls who more readily succeeded in attracting the young man's attention was one who was also quite beautiful, occupying a box not very far away from his. As always happens with girls who are truly ingenuous—not with that conventional ingenuousness they must assume like a role in a comedy until a husband authorizes them to play a different role, but with that true ingenuousness which has its roots in virginity of the mind and heart—she was immediately and deeply affected by him. She was too young to know how to feign it, really, and I believe I was not alone in noticing her agitation and excitement.

For a short time I witnessed the mysterious rapport that was established between them, and like an intruder, I thrust myself into the magnetic current formed by their gazes. Then, as if feeling ashamed of my spying, of my winking at their happiness, like a beggar who attends a banquet from the threshold of the dining room and can only enjoy the smells of the sauces and viands, I withdrew into myself and managed to turn my complete attention to the performance of the opera.

I say that I felt ashamed, but only for myself. If there is anything in the world before which I can neither sneer with disdain nor weep with pity, it is the sight of two people who love each other. Often at night I have strolled down public paths, through a thicket of linden trees, purposely to meet some enamored couples; and I have never passed by one without feeling myself seized by one without feeling myself seized by a sentiment of profound respect. I confess that those have been the only moments in my life when my fellows seemed to me less sad than usual.

I had gradually succeeded in devoting myself entirely to the performance and no longer raised my eyes toward that unknown man's box when, perceiving a sudden movement in the audience and noticing the crowd thronging toward the door, I too moved and reached the lobby with difficulty. There I saw two gentlemen bearing away a girl who had fainted, transporting her to one of the rooms in the theater.

I will not mention my astonishment in recognizing her as the same girl who had looked at my unknown man with so much affection and persistence. Everything that happened could have been no more than a freak of chance; yet it was the second time within a period of two hours that I had seen a person he regarded with fondness suddenly struck down by some misfortune.

I returned to the orchestra.

He was still occupying his seat; he had stayed in the same position as before, his cheek resting on his hand. Yet his face, after a sudden, bright red flush, turned instantly to a cadaverous paleness. It was not difficult to notice that he was suffering, aware of the curious, almost reproachful glances fixed on him, and he remained motionless in his seat only to dissemble his agitation, avoiding any acknowledgement of his peculiar complicity in that incident.

When the crowd appeared to shift its attention away from him, he left the theater, and I too left.

Perhaps no one knew of the much more lamentable incident that had taken place a few hours earlier; perhaps no one remarked on the singular and incomprehensible circumstance of that void he seemed to form around himself, nor did anyone give thought to the relations that seemed to join all these facts. I, however, was constantly thinking of them. He obviously possessed something inexplicable and fatal.

I had seen him alone in the center of a space formed almost

miraculously amidst an extremely dense crowd, and I had seen the same phenomenon repeated in a theater filled with spectators. I had seen a boy who received his caresses run down by the wheels of a carriage, and a girl he noticed overcome by a sudden malaise. The idea that a simple coincidence caused this series of events seemed impossible to me. And if it were not a coincidence, then who was he? What influence could this man exercise?

Eight days later, I was in Café Martini—that haunt of painters who never paint, singers who never sing, writers who never write, and elegant people who are always penniless. Quite a few of them were sitting around a table talking about some sort of newly invented pie, something similar to a pudding, which that night had been added to the restaurant's menu.

The conversation turned from this subject, and after passing through the idea of pudding and the goose the wealthy classes in London used to give the poor on Christmas day, it arrived at the speech the queen of England had recently delivered in parliament.

A sentence from this speech gave a powerful shot to the discussion and on the return volley drove it to the possibility of war in Italy. From there, bouncing down the slope of personal opinions and foresight, it reached predictions; from predictions it rolled to presentiments; and from presentiments it entered the court of spiritual life, stopping at fate, sorcery, and spells; so that five minutes after the excellence of the new pie had been vigorously defended, I was relating to this group of idlers what I had witnessed a few days ago—the incomprehensible events involving the unknown young man.

Needless to say, they laughed and refused to believe me. The girl's fainting that night had become rather well known, but the causes, they said, must be different. Nonetheless, the subject of this new turn in our discourse was found interesting, and the conversation, after wavering over so many topics, settled firmly on this one. Everyone set forth his own ideas, everyone had something to tell in this connection. And as happens whenever we face the frightening world of the incomprehensible and supernatural—we mock it at the outset to show off our courage but end up terrified by what we hear, often by what we ourselves relate—each of us felt possessed by a mixture of fear and amazement. Whenever the conversation showed any signs of languishing, moreover, we did our utmost to renew and rekindle it with the insatiability children have for listening to terrifying tales of witches and fairies.

We had nearly exhausted our entire repertoire of ideas on this thesis, when an old actor whom we had all known for some time—one of the most celebrated caryatids in that café—stood up at the nearby table where he had been listening and came to take a chair in our group.

"The gentleman is right," he said, pointing at me. "I do not know the young man he spoke of a little while ago, and I cannot corroborate the influence he attributes to him, but the fact that men exist who are fatal in such a way—indeed, much more fatal than that young man—nothing can call into question. Have any of you heard the name of Count Corrado di Sagrezwitch?"

No one had.

"That is strange, since he has acquired a terrible reputation in almost every country in Europe and many of the United States. He is considered the most fatal man in memory: his presence anywhere signals an inevitable misfortune. He is always found on the scene of the most terrible calamities, and he has witnessed the most frightening disasters. He was in South America when the church in San Iago burned and more than a thousand people perished; he was traveling two years ago on the Pacific Railroad when that collision occurred in which more than three hundred passengers lost their lives; he was at Saint Petersburg when the palace of Prince Yakorliff collapsed and many noblewomen and state dignitaries were found dead. In the mines of Ireland and those of Alstau Moor in Scotland—places that he has often visited—his name is never heard without fear; each of his visits signaled some of the catastrophes that have been so frequent and so dreaded in the mines. Count Sagrezwitch has already traveled in Italy on several occasions. He is thought to have been in Turin during September of 1864, when the Convention that the government signed with Napoleon III to withdraw French troops ultimately precipitated a tragic uprising. Yet no one, as far as I know, saw him there."

"And do you know him?"

"I have met him four times in my travels. You know that as an actor and theatrical impresario I have covered almost all of Europe and a good bit of the New World. This is perhaps how I could be aware of the extraordinary man's existence and know him personally. The first time I saw him was in Berlin, where I made my debut in the title role of Mozart's masterpiece, *Don Giovanni*. Then I encountered him in a coffeehouse in New York, when the war of secession was still raging in America, exactly on the eve of the separatists' ultimate defeat. The third time was again in Berlin—"

"Where was he born?"

"Some say he is American, others Polish. No one knows his native country with certainty, perhaps not even his name. In America he is known as the Duke of Nevers; in Europe I always heard the name Count Sagrezwitch; the Scottish miners called him 'the fatal man.' He is fluent in many languages and has assimilated the habits and customs of all the countries he has visited: in Italy he is Italian, in England English, and in America he is the model American . . ."

"How old can he be?"

"He appears to be about fifty, but his jet black hair and beard do not show the slightest trace of age. He is a man of medium height, with a disagreeable look, although his features are normal and rather elegant. In the winter he almost always wears a fur hat shaped like a turban, and as a rule he readily dons the dress of any country where he finds himself. To judge from the way he usually squanders his money, one would say that he is very wealthy. Nonetheless, on several occasions he has been seen lodging at second-rate inns and maintaining a very frugal way of life. In New York, for example, he certainly stayed at the Fifth Avenue Hotel, that marble colossus containing twelve hundred rooms, but he occupied a bed in the waiting area provided for travelers who have extremely limited means at their disposal. It is reported that he is aware of his fatal influence and takes pleasure in exercising it. His continual traveling from one corner of the globe to the other cannot be fortuitous. It is known, however, that he has no lovers, no friends, perhaps not even any acquaintances, except for a few, very superficial relationships. Those who know of his power avoid him deliberately; those who are ignorant of it, instinctively." The actor paused, seeing that several of us were smiling with an air of incredulity, then resumed. "That some people deny him this power, this sort of mysterious and terrible mission, is a most natural thing. No one can prove that the misfortunes which occurred in the places he happened to be, and at the times he happened to be there, found their cause in his will, or in what we call his influence. He is, furthermore, a man like all others; he talks, dresses, acts like every other man, and there is nothing that opposes our describing him as affable and gentlemanly. Yet it seems to me blindness to deny what the majority of men has admitted, and particularly to deny it because it is not understood."

"It is not that we deny," I told him, "we doubt. Incidentally, you forgot to tell us where you met him the fourth time."

"Ah!" he began again, somewhat reassured by my words. "This last encounter has a very recent date. I saw him two months ago in London, when the queen's theater burned. In fact, I know that he was intending to pass through Italy soon, and if he chose this season to travel here, it seems quite likely that the festivities at carnival would have led him to Milan."

"To Milan!"

"Yes, and I wish that you could see him. I cannot tell you the motive for this wish, but it seems to me that the mere sight of him would help you to understand so many things I am unable to explain to you. And you could no longer doubt the truth of my assertions . . . You would observe," he resumed after several moments, "something very remarkable in his dress—I mean the freshness and fineness of his gloves, which he used to change so many times in a single day that no one has ever seen his bare hands. His appearance is distinguished by another singularity that is no less noteworthy—namely, the power of his gaze. It possesses a magnetic, inexplicable quality that virtually compels you to stare and greet him in spite of yourself."

"Greet him!" we exclaimed, smiling.

"Yes, greet him."

"Oh, I would like to see him!"

"Indeed!"

"We shall see him!"

At that instant—it could have been two in the morning—the door of the café opened, and a large, heavyset man entered the room. Given the portrait just sketched for us, with the fur hat, the hands sheathed in the most spotless gloves, the singular facial expression, we did not take long to recognize him as the man who had been the subject of our conversation. Then—it was either amazement or confusion caused by that surprise—we all stood up at once to greet him. He raised his hand to his hat in a courteous gesture that was sincere yet restrained, and he took a seat at the other end of the room.

I cannot express the confusion, amazement, and irritation which overcame us at that moment. We realized that we appeared weak to him, to ourselves, and perhaps ridiculous. Everybody remained absorbed in this thought, nor did anyone dare resume the conversation. The silence increased our confusion.

The unknown man asked for a cup of punch, which he drank eagerly. He threw a silver scudo on the tray and gave the waiter the change from the price of his drink. When the waiter turned to walk away, he tripped over one of the back legs of the man's chair and fell. The tray slipped from his hand, and he struck his face against the shards of the cup, which had broken, cutting himself in such a way that he was instantly covered with blood.

At that sight we all rose as if moved by a single will and rushed headlong from the room.

In the early days of my residence in Milan, I was forced, almost against my wishes, to become acquainted with a family who had years ago rendered me some very useful services through the mediation of friends. They were living in one of those gray, isolated hovels that flanked the canal on the western side of the city—an old house with two floors which the roof seemed to compress and squeeze together like a heavy leaden weight, so low and narrow were they. All around it stood some black, worm-eaten boards that supported dwarfish pumpkins and convolvulus ailing with chlorosis.

Day and night a nearby silk factory wrapped the house in a cloud of smoke, while the dampness from the canal stained the exterior plaster of the walls and covered them with mold and small sorrel plants. Swarms of flies entered one's mouth and nose as soon as one looked out the window; and the chattering, beating, and singing of the laundresses who rinsed and hung out their wash on the boards with the pumpkins created a continual, deafening uproar from morning to night.

Perhaps less than a hundred people live in the center of Milan, and they know this part of its outskirts with precision. Milan is the exact miniature of a huge metropolis; it has everything that is characteristic of the great capitals, but in small proportions. That last strip of houses which skirted the canal from Porta Nuova to Porta Ticinese is what the Marinella is to Naples, the Temple to Paris, and the Seven Dials to London.

Averse to knowing new things and people—partly by instinct, partly by design—I have always considered a new acquaintance as a new burden placed on my life. This one, however, I have not regretted. The family consisted of honest merchants who moderately prospered in business and had come to live in that solitary house so as to enjoy in peace the small fortune they had scraped together.

Silvia, the only heir to that fortune, was one of the most dazzling beauties I have ever seen, and she was only seventeen when I met her. She was not one of those delicate, refined beauties that we often prefer to robust ones—for several years now, love has taken a giant step toward spiritualism—but her beauty, although ineffably serene, although blooming with all the graces of youth and health, was tempered by a kind, thoughtful quality that beauties of this sort ordinarily do not possess. I can say no more about it; each of us carries a different ideal of beauty within himself, and when it is said that a woman is lovely, everything that can be said about her has been said. A painter or sculptor could provide a less partial image with their art; literature cannot—the other arts speak to the senses, literature to the mind. I have seen two engravings by Jubert, two angels symbolized by two adolescent girls, nude, plump, rosy: the vividness and fullness of their figures make them true women of the people. And yet the artist could endow those faces with so much spirituality that they were bewitching and one was unable to look at them without being enraptured. In Carraccio's Madonnas, I have observed the same contrast. Silvia's beauty was of this sort, and in a sense it resolved the same problem—the spirituality of matter.

She was one of those simple, pious, modest souls who never know any rancor in their lives, rich in that charming frivolity which nature has dispensed so liberally to women, happy in the order and quiet that their own simplicity has created around themselves, and that their want of passion can never disturb.

During my first visits to Silvia's family, I met one of her cousins, a certain Davide, a mature, practical young man who had arrived in Milan not long ago and was for a time concerned with the financial affairs of the house. He was threatening like all cousins

—I do not know whether equally fortunate—and it was difficult for me to admit that he was flirting with the girl. Like all other men, he was neither handsome nor ugly. Male beauty is a cipher whose code has still not been broken; even for the majority of women, it remains insignificant. In men we look for character; women seek simply a man—they are the authors of that well-known aphorism: a man is always handsome.

I confess that my discovery was one of the essential reasons I neglected my acquaintance with this family. I had not set my sights on Silvia's dowry or beauty, but I understood that Davide's love, which I believed was reciprocated, cast me in a certain inferior light, and I felt humiliated. In any man who approaches a woman, one assumes the desire to court her; in two men approaching her at the same time, one supposes the virtual duty to struggle in order to win her favor. At least society and the human heart continue to harbor such prejudices; lexicons may have changed, but things and passions have not: every circle of women still comprises a small, intimate court of love where courteous weapons battle for the affection of a favored lady. And then I have always felt so inadequate in the presence of a practical man that I have never had sufficient spirit to engage in any struggle with such an enemy. What is a scholar, a man of letters, a sage, compared to what we call a man of the world? Intellect is still such a small thing! How much do ignorant men, with their common sense, bourgeois, crude, trivial, how much do they advance us in science and the knowledge of things! We can only stumble like children over the smallest obstacles in life!

This awareness of my inferiority, then, rendered my visits less frequent (in the very city where I now live I am acquainted with families I visit every three or four years, as though I were returning from a voyage circumnavigating the globe). Later, after the death of Silvia's father, the one person in that family to whom I was especially obligated, I found an excuse to break off the relationship completely.

Thus, nearly a year had passed when, a few days after the singular appearance of Count Sagrezwitch at Café Martini, I ran into Davide, whom I had not seen for some time. He seemed much changed.

He grasped my hands and looked at me with a sad, troubled expression—that mixture of reserve and confidence possessed by people who want you to realize they have a painful secret, which, however, they do not want to confide in you.

"You have made yourself scarce at my cousin's house," he said to me. "Your sudden absence caused a rather painful shock in that family. You know that my aunt put trust in you, and then . . . she had gotten into the habit of seeing you. If only you knew! New misfortunes have befallen that house; Silvia is about to die—"

"About to die!"

"Yes, the poor girl is suffering from a wasting disease, some mysterious illness that the doctors can neither understand nor describe precisely, but they have declared it incurable. She is going to marry—"

"You, perhaps?"

"Not me," he said sadly, "a rich foreigner, to whom I was subordinated. She conceived a passion for him that I never would have thought her capable of. She was planning to marry him when she fell ill, and this wedding, even if it is performed now as I believe they have resolved, can never have any influence on her health. I doubt that happiness has the power to make her live any longer. At least she will be happy for those few moments of life she has left. She will also be happy without me," he added with bitterness. "It is not difficult to see that she deteriorates every day, and the course of this deterioration, so rapid and mysterious, is impossible to stop."

"How can this be?" I asked. "Will she marry that man even when she is sick as you tell me?"

Davide shook his head with an air of disapproval and replied, "What do you want! This is what they have chosen to do; in fact, it was she herself who made the decision. Her illness, however, is not the kind that forces her to remain in bed, but rather one of those of which we say, she is dying on her feet. But why not come to visit us? I am certain that my aunt would be very pleased to see you, and Silvia as well."

"Are you going there now?"

"Yes."

I accompanied him. It must have been ten at night when we set foot in that house. Davide's aunt, a good old woman—age and childhood meet: the elderly are always as good as children—welcomed me with a joyfulness that was genuine and cordial, but tempered somewhat by reproach and melancholy.

"You will find us much changed," she told me. "You have not come to my home for some time . . . poor Silvia . . ." And she stopped for a moment as if to pause over the thought of that misfortune. "But come in here, you can see her for yourself, it will please her. And I shall introduce you to my son-in-law."

We entered the next room.

Silvia was sitting in an armchair, a large chair on castors, which was completely upholstered in a deep blue velvet; next to her, on a lower chair, sat the unknown young man I had seen at the carnival procession and the theater. He had drawn up his chair close enough to the girl's to be able to lay his head on the same armrest where she laid her arm, while her head was bowed over the young man's in a gesture of moving tenderness.

God! How much she had changed! It was scarcely possible to recognize her. The girl I had seen so healthy, so relaxed, so vivacious was no more than a shadow of the past, no more than a pale, uncertain reflection of her former beauty. It was not that her loveliness had entirely vanished, but it was altered; it was now a different loveliness, the beauty of a flower that bloomed in the shade, of a fruit that ripened too early and was worm-eaten. The young man's face was pale, but Silvia's was white, whiter than the long, gauzy gown that wrapped her body, except that her slightly sunken cheeks were light pink, but without shading, as if two faded rose leaves had been placed upon them. Her hair had that dull sheen which the hair of the sick ordinarily has, and it hung, not loose, but disheveled, over the head of the young man who was gazing at her with a look of inexpressible pity.

His pallor, although extreme, was not the kind that accompanies illness, but habitual thought and anguish. He was even more handsome than he had seemed in the theater—and this time I could judge at close quarters—with a beauty more feminine than masculine, but in any case more beautiful. His blond, nearly golden hair made a strange contrast mingled that way with the girl's jet black tresses. I had never seen such an astonishing couple, or a portrait of love that was more spiritual or pure.

The two lovers stirred at the creak of the opening door—they were alone in the room.

"Look, Silvia," her mother said sweetly, taking me by the hand, "look who your cousin brought back with him."

And turning toward the unknown man and me, she pronounced first my name, then his, which she said was Baron Saternez, a native of Pilsen in Bohemia.

We bowed to one another. He gazed at me so pleasantly that I placed my hand on him nearly without realizing it.

After we exchanged a few words, the old woman, perhaps to leave the two young people alone, drew me near her in an opposite corner of the room.

"What does my son-in-law seem like to you?" she asked me. Then she continued without waiting for my reply, "He is a proper young man, you know, rich as the sea; if only you saw the gifts he gave Silvia! . . . And then his family! Barons, and among the most renowned in Bohemia. He had to emigrate for political reasons; I believe that he wanted Bohemia to be annexed to the Grand Duchy of Saxony—imagine that! But it made no difference in the end: he lost interest in staying in his country, since he was the last surviving member of his family. And look at what a handsome young man he is. Do not be offended"—she looked at me as if to interrogate me; I smiled—"do not be offended, but I cannot believe the world contains another man like that one. And to think—" The old woman interrupted herself as if suddenly struck by a sad thought.

"Poor Silvia!" she resumed after a few moments. "You have seen her before today, you remember how she was! And now!

Look at her. Only four months have passed since she started wasting away like this; it began the day my son-in-law entered our home. She could be so happy now; they love each other so much! Tell me, do you think she will ever recover?"

"There is no reason to doubt it," I answered to comfort her. "Until now Silvia has lived such a retired, quiet, calm life that this unusual disorder in her affections has caused a slight disturbance in her health as well. But it will all end when everything returns to a normal state, when they are husband and wife. Speaking of which, I heard from your nephew that it will occur very soon."

"In eight days," said the old woman, "and I hope that you will be with us on that occasion. They are the ones who wanted it like this, and the doctors have not disapproved. Silvia is still strong enough to bear the ride to the church in the carriage; besides, we are not very far away . . . The celebration will be a little sad," she added, pressing my hand, "but you cannot refuse to be a part of it."

I thanked her and assured her that I would come. I spent the remainder of that night troubled by strange, tumultuous thoughts, divided between the irresistible sympathy that Silvia's fiancé inspired in me and the repugnance that I increasingly felt at the idea of the fatal mission he seemed to be executing. There was no longer any question: that young man, so handsome, pleasant, attractive, strewed desolation and misfortune about himself, left frightening traces in his path. Every creature he was especially fond of succumbed to his influence—the boy with the maskers, the lady in the theater, Silvia, that very Silvia who was once so beautiful, so carefree, so flourishing bore witness to his terrible power. And whether or not he was aware of it, this power was not less real or deadly. Warning his victims, delivering them from that man's incomprehensible influence, was both a duty and an act of compassion.

I left the house near midnight. Davide accompanied me. My heart was full. We set off for the city walls without uttering a word.

The night was cold but dry; the horse chestnuts with their black bark and their tall, slender trunks seemed like specters of trees; the sky, as happens on clear winter nights, sparkled with myriad stars. It did not take me long to notice that my companion's spirit was also deeply troubled.

"Let us sit down," I said to him, pointing to a stone bench. "I must reveal to you several things that concern our cousin."

And at length I related to him everything I observed regarding Baron Saternez. I did not conceal my suspicions; I spoke of Count Sagrezwitch and the encounter we had at Café Martini, and I concluded by urging him to do his utmost in order to avert the misfortune threatening that house.

"I am grateful to you," he answered, after having listened to me very attentively. "That wedding will not occur, I give you my word. I hesitated up to this point, but now—"

"How do you intend to oppose it?"

"I do not know, but you shall see," and he added in a terrible voice, "No, that wedding will not happen. I, I myself shall make it impossible . . . because . . . it must not happen, because I am the one who should enjoy that happiness, because I detest that man, because it is he who stole Silvia's love from me . . . because I hate him!"

Early the next morning Davide came to find me at my house. He was calm, but with that cold, convulsive calm which spreads like a veil over one's features when reflection has already concentrated the entire struggle in the heart. The tempests of the human heart are like those at sea: the least apparent are the most intense.

"I come," he told me, "to ask for more information regarding the revelations you made to me last night. I thought about them all night and did not close my eyes. I need to know where Count Sagrezwitch lives and whether he is still in Milan. Perhaps you can tell me."

"I do not know," I replied, amazed. "But what are you planning to do? Do you perhaps intend to visit him? To what end?"

"You spoke to me," he resumed, "of the deadly influence these two men exercise, he and Baron Saternz, and their power to do evil through ways other than those granted to us, whether or not they are conscious of it. The count, you told me, possesses this power to a greater extent. Now, whatever the causes of this influence may be, whatever its nature, if it exists and if they do not possess it in equal amounts, have you thought of the consequences that would result from the impact of these two forces, from the meeting of these two fatal men? Put them face-to-face, and if this power truly exists, one must destroy the other; the disparity of the forces will cause an imbalance. The defeat of the weaker one is inevitable."

"That is a rather specious argument," I said. "You must have thought, then—"

"About arranging for Count Sagrezwitch to be in the presence of my rival."

"Do you intend to speak to the count?"

"If only I could find him. This is why I have come to you, and I am distressed that you are unable to give me the information I need . . . But I shall find him, yes, I shall find him," he continued resolutely. "Milan has only a few elegant hotels where he may have taken a room; I shall search through them all, I shall ask for him at every door, and if he is still here or if he departed a short time ago, I shall not despair of picking up his trail."

No sooner had Davide said this than he hurried out of the

room, before my astonishment and hesitation about whether to encourage or dissuade him from that project permitted me to utter a word.

I spent that entire day filled with a mortal uneasiness.

That night, at a very late hour, I received a letter from Davide which reads as follows:

At this moment I am leaving for Genoa, where I shall join my family in a small village on the coast. I have pondered this plan for a long time without being able to make up my mind. The events that have already occurred and those about to occur have finally driven me to make this decision. I have no wish to remain here to let compassion divert me from my vendetta—assuming that I still have the power to stop it—nor to let the sight of its accomplishment, whatever that may be, overwhelm me with regrets I should not have. I feel the need to tell you everything I have done for Silvia's salvation. There was no selfishness in this effort; her heart no longer belonged to me, nor did I want to claim it again; I wanted only her happiness. My disinterestedness will appear more sincere with the renunciation I shall make of my cousin's hand, even when her heart is free and her youth flourishing again.

I cannot tell you any more. I found Count Sagrezwitch, and I spoke to him. Those two men know each other. I have no part at all in what is about to happen; remember it well. I can neither foresee nor stop the events that must occur; it was the hand of fate that planned them. I was no more than their instrument: I approached two men who should have remained far from each other—this was my entire responsibility; and it is my love for Silvia that drove me to undertake the burden. May my justification remain forever in your memory! It is impossible for me to explain myself any further. Destroy this letter at once.

Never in my life have I been involved in a sadder and more complicated plot. What were Davide's needs? What had he said to Count Sagrezwitch? How could he talk to me with so much certainty about a vendetta that had to be executed without him? And why had he left? Even Silvia's salvation, if such a thing were still possible, did not console me in my regret at having confided Baron Saternez's secret to Davide and at putting the latter in a position to avenge himself. I was obligated to remedy, if I could, the evil I had done. Only seven days remained before the date set for the wedding, and this vendetta, whose goal was to prevent it, had to be accomplished in the interval.

I resolved to visit the young baron and, according to his responses to my insinuations, confide everything in him or let him suspect the danger that threatened him. I destroyed Davide's letter; and availing myself of the address he had given me for his rival, I immediately went to his house.

Baron Saternez did not show the slightest surprise at seeing me; he took my hand with an affectionate gesture that exceeded simple courtesy and said, "I was expecting you."

"What do you mean?" I exclaimed, astonished. "Then you know the reason for my visit?"

"Yes," he said. And after a moment of silence, he replied with a fierce smile. "I am not only a dangerous man; I am also an experienced physiognomist. When I saw you for the first time the day before yesterday, I divined that your heart was good, and that if you ever erred through weakness or good intentions, you would not hesitate to grieve over the consequences of your errors and endeavor to make amends. As a result of your friend's visit, Count Sagrezwitch was here two hours ago. It was therefore natural for me to expect you."

I bowed my head and said nothing.

After another moment of silence, he resumed. "Do not worry about what you did, and do not reproach Davide for the evils he has prepared. What will happen must happen. You were no more than a tool in the hands of fate. The sentiments that moved you to impede my actions are praiseworthy, although perhaps useless; I am not so unjust as to ignore them. That man and I knew each other for quite some time; perhaps we even sought each other." He pronounced these words more emphatically. "He and I are linked by relations that nature or chance created almost in mockery, terrible relations that a secret forbids me from revealing to you. Our meeting was inevitable because it was predestined. It was necessary for one of us to die, because two antagonistic elements cannot meet without struggling; they cannot travel the same path, cannot walk side by side, as if they had only a common power to exercise, a common mission to carry out. You were right to do what you did. It is fortune that directed you. It was long overdue!"

He broke off, then resumed after another moment of silence in which I did not dare speak. "Look at me! You see in me a man like all others, perhaps seemingly better than others. My person does not inspire disgust; my face, my behavior, that part of the soul which nature has placed in our features as if to reveal the powers hidden in the heart do not possess anything odious, anything that is not human, not pleasant, perhaps not even attractive. Well, this young man who you would have judged innocuous, whose friendship you would perhaps have desired without knowing him, has strewn ruin and desolation about himself, killed people who loved him, undermined the life and happiness of everyone who knew and cared for him. Because . . . yes, you guessed, you grasped his secret. Until now, this man, this wretch," he proceeded with growing excitement, "has never had the power to relinquish an existence that made so many people unhappy; this is his crime. He was born for the good. Nature set the image of the good before his eyes like a brilliant ideal, like a sweet, shining goal. He would have liked to love, to perform good deeds, to rejoice at the happiness he sowed about himself, to lay a crown on the head of every man . . . but a cruel, terrible, ineluctable destiny condemned him to do evil, to crush beneath the burden of his fate all those good, affectionate beings who surrounded him."

He fell silent and covered his face with his hands.

"Calm yourself," I said. "If you have this power, you certainly exaggerate its significance."

He smiled as if to show that he would indulge my doubt, then resumed. "No, I have not exaggerated. You would agree if you could return to the beginnings of my life to discover the signs I left behind and judge their depth and extent. My own childhood—the age when everybody is happy—was nothing but a period of sadness and pain for me. The creatures who loved me most began to succumb; my brothers, my sisters, my mother died; I began to notice the void that gaped around me, and I understood that there was something fatal in my destiny. Very soon I was alone in the world. The more I saw the circle of my relations, affections, and sympathies widen, the more I saw that void widen; the more I entered into life, the more I found myself isolated. I felt the need for friendship, felt the fever of love . . . yet friends and lovers vanished into the abyss I dug for them at my feet. I began to be assailed by a frightening doubt: was I fatal to everyone I loved, to everyone who loved me? I went back over my past, retraced the path of my existence step by step, interrogated all the ruins in my wake . . . It was true—belief was inescapable—it was terribly true! Then I left my native country and wandered through the world, fleeing, and fleeing myself. The misfortune that struck down the people I loved most showered me with riches at the cost of their lives, although I alone could avail myself of these riches, although no one could ever benefit from me with impunity. It was thus that roaming from country to country I came to Milan, that fleeing the crowd and society to render myself less fatal, frequenting the most humble and remote districts, I met Silvia and was irresistibly taken with her before the awareness of the evil I would cause had the power to divert me from that affection. She requited me. I was young, unfortunate, entitled to give love and ask for it—I who never felt happiness, who did nothing but steal it from others without being able to enjoy it myself, who always had to fling it away like a bitter, forbidden fruit. You know the rest. You know that I am now threatened by danger, and you come to apprise me of it. Well, it is too late—the goal of my life is attained. If death must strike me down, I can no longer find anything bitter or unpleasant in it: I have realized the end of my aspirations, and I smile at the impotence of those who would like to prevent it."

He uttered these words with a kind of loftiness that invested a countenance already so gentle with a singularly severe expression.

"Yes, you are too late," he continued with enthusiasm. "You would have liked to prevent my wedding. Well, know that this wedding is no more than a pretense staged for society, a justification for what love has already given spontaneously. Silvia was mine! What does it matter that she must die? And what is dying? Did love ever have a different aspiration? Did it ever have any other recompense than this? Whether I am too early or too late, I now invoke this death you wanted to arrange for me."

"Oh, not I!" I exclaimed. "Heaven is my witness if I desired or planned your death. You forget that I am here at this very moment to warn you of a danger, certainly not to threaten you with it."

"It is true," he answered softly. "Forgive me." And he placed a hand on me, but withdrew it immediately, as if he were afraid of offending or harming me with that contact.

I looked into his face to examine it. It was so handsome, so peaceful; it had again become so nobly calm. There was something so virile in his childlike face and so strong in his very weakness that I understood how a woman could accept his love even at the cost of her life. I was unaware of whether Silvia knew the young man's secret, but I felt that even if she did know it, the sacrifice of her existence must have appeared to her an extremely paltry thing compared to the sweetness of that love.

He may have known the power of his beauty or read it in my heart, since he offered me his hand a second time and told me, "Go, go, I beseech you. You are kind, perhaps you can feel some sympathy for me, whereas I am likely to reward with ingratitude the service you wanted to render me with your visit. It is my destiny!—"

"It may still be such," I interrupted, "I am not afraid." And I seized his hand and clasped it to my heart. "I judged you different; I wanted to prevent a misfortune. It was all my fault."

"Do not torment yourself with this thought," he said. "I am not a man who can believe in the freedom of human actions—free will is a lie—the will is only the foreknowledge of an act that is already preordained; it does not have any weight on the scale where everything in life is weighed—the scale of destiny."

I shook my head doubtfully. He observed that gesture and resumed. "No, I shall not attempt to avert that danger in any way; it would be pointless. I thank you, in any case."

"Will I see you again?" I asked, almost uncertain of whether to leave him so firm in his resolve.

He smiled with an expression of gratitude and said, "When would you like—tomorrow?"

"Tomorrow."

I omit the account of my relations with Baron Saternez during those seven days that preceded his wedding. It was due to them that I could develop a less imprecise idea of his character, although he never allowed me to fathom the mystery of his life any more than was possible during our first meeting. Nonetheless, I learned enough to be able to form an opinion concerning him. He was undoubtedly honest, undoubtedly good. I have known few men who presented a more singular mixture of weakness and strength in their temperament—I mean that weakness which resides in sensitivity, in the disposition to receive impressions powerfully, not in feebleness of character. He had a skeptical mind and a believing heart; misfortune did not debilitate him, but it made him old before his time, so that he appeared young or old at intervals, according to the internal impulse he received from his passions. And although he seemed naturally demonstrative like all good people, he actually was not. Perhaps the sad power with which he believed himself endowed taught him to hide and dissimulate. From that day onward, in any case, no matter how much fondness he showed for me, he never again lifted the veil which spread over his past, and which he had partly lifted in that first effusive moment.

In those days, it seemed to me that his temperament was not as melancholy as I had first judged, yet later I easily noticed that his joy possessed something violent, forced, convulsive, and he lived under the apprehension of a thought that filled him with terror. He passed from excesses of hilarity to excesses of sadness;

he often seemed calm and feigned a peace of mind he did not feel. But that was for Silvia's benefit. She loved him with that species of blindness which sees nothing at all.

He took long walks with me in those days, and in the countryside he pointed out several prospects and effects of light and snow that would have escaped a mind neither poetic nor observant. He showed no fear of the danger about which I had spoken to him, and he made no allusion to it with me, yet he visibly paled whenever he heard the count's name mentioned. One night—only two days remained before the nuptials—I was surprised to meet him in the company of Count Sagrezwitch on a dark, remote path. I followed them but did not manage to comprehend a single word of their lively, animated dialogue. They spoke a language I did not know; and it seemed to me from the count's gestures and imperious tone that he was insisting on a request with which the baron obstinately refused to comply.

After that night, it became obvious that the baron was trying to anesthetize himself from some great anxiety with any means possible. He turned to wine to forget his secret pain, and on the following day I myself led him back to his house in a very serious state of intoxication.

But I shall abbreviate my narrative.

The wedding day arrived, and the wedding itself was completed without the emergence of any obstacle to stop it. An informal family party took place that evening; a great many of the bride's relatives and friends were present.

Silvia was radiant; Baron Saternez was so youthfully happy that I privately rejoiced at the vanity of Davide's threats and perhaps also of the young man's alleged influence, in which I tried to stop believing. It seemed to me that the prospect of such great happiness had to restore the girl's health and destroy in him that terrible, mysterious power with which he believed himself endowed.

Midnight had already passed, and I was thinking, seated in a corner of the room, that these possibilities might lie in the newlyweds' future, when I heard the Duke of Nevers mentioned near me. I immediately remembered that this was the name which Count Sagrezwitch often used in America. I was startled and turned around. A servant entered the room and presented to the bridegroom a calling card which bore that name surmounted by a ducal crown. The strange visitor had to speak to Baron Saternez at once and was waiting for him in the vestibule.

"It is a pressing matter," the young man said without manifesting even the slightest emotion. "In fact . . . I needed to speak to that man. I shall return in a few minutes."

He squeezed Silvia's hand and went down. When the door was opened, I seemed to glimpse Count Sagrezwitch at the rear of the vestibule, but I could not affirm it. The servant who saw him said afterwards, however, that the person who had himself announced as the Duke of Nevers wore a very large fur hat and kid gloves of an immaculate whiteness.

We waited for the baron all night—a cold, rainy March night—but in vain. I forego describing the family's distress; it would be a task greater than words. The next day the reports in the newspapers read: "A young foreigner who resided for some time in our city, where he arrived with a false passport in the name of Baron Saternez, a Bohemian, but whose real name is Gustav of the counts of Sagrezwitch, a Pole, was found dead this morning behind the walls of Porta Tenaglia, with a knife plunged in his heart. The circumstances and the agents of this murder remain unknown."

Now, what were the bonds that linked those two men and those two names? What were their real names? Had one of them usurped the other's name, or did they both use it? And the Duke of Nevers! Was this truly the surname of Sagrezwitch who asserted that he knew the young man and with whom the latter said he had some relations he could not reveal? It is an enigma that neither I nor any of the people to whom I have told this story could ever resolve.

Silvia, however, recovered—whether by chance or because of the nature of the illness, she recovered, although her wounded heart never healed. Her family sold their gray, musty house and settled in the small village of Brianza. The man known by the name of Count Sagrezwitch was never seen again in Milan. I have not heard anything more of Davide.

Two years have passed from the date of this incident, and no light has been shed on the crime.

[1869]

archipelago books
is a not-for-profit literary press devoted to
promoting cross-cultural exchange through innovative
classic and contemporary international literature
www.archipelagobooks.org